The BRUISE

The BRUISE

MAGDALENA ZURAWSKI

FC2

TUSCALOOSA

The University of Alabama Press
Tuscaloosa, Alabama 35487-0380

First Edition

Published by FC2, an imprint of the University of Alabama Press, with support provided by Florida State University, the Publications Unit of the Department of English at Illinois State University, and the School of Arts and Sciences, University of Houston–Victoria

Address all editorial inquiries to: Fiction Collective Two, University of Houston–Victoria, School of Arts and Sciences, Victoria, TX 77901-5731

⊗

The paper on which this book is printed meets the minimum requirements of American National Standard for Information Sciences—Permanence of Paper for Printed Library Materials, ANSI Z39.48–1984

Library of Congress Cataloging-in-Publication Data
Zurawski, Magdalena.
The bruise / by Magdalena Zurawski. — 1st ed.
p. cm.
ISBN-13: 978-1-57366-144-7 (pbk. : alk. paper)
ISBN-10: 1-57366-144-9 (pbk. : alk. paper)
1. Women college students—Fiction. 2. Dreams—Fiction. I. Title.
PS3576.U543B78 2008
813'.54—dc22

2007049000

Book Design: Stephen Shoup and Tara Reeser
Cover Design: Lou Robinson
Typeface: Garamond
Produced and printed in the United States of America

Acknowledgements

Many thanks to the editors of the following journals and anthologies in which some of these chapters first appeared: *Bay Poetics*, *Eleven Eleven*, *EOAGH*, *The Hat*, *Narrativity*, *No: A Journal of the Arts*, and *SHAMPOO*. And to Suzanne Stein, who published a selection of the work as a TAXT chapbook.

Much thanks to Yaddo and the Millay Colony for the Arts for supporting the writing of this book through residencies. And to the Temple University Creative Writing Department for awarding me the Joseph Beam Scholarship Prize, which helped fund the writing of this book.

Special thanks to Alan Singer, who helped me start this project, and Emily Carner, who helped me finish it.

For advice and encouragement along the way I'd like to thank the Zurawski family, Kate Pringle, CAConrad, Frank Sherlock, Aaron Kunin, Renee Gladman, Robert Glück, Gail Scott, Adeena Karasick, Ben Lerner, David Buuck, Rosmarie and Keith Waldrop, Laynie Brown, Peter Gizzi, Amanda Davidson, Prageeta Sharma, Kelly Marshall, Elise Ficarra, Jen Scappetone, Judith Goldman, and Jocelyn Saidenberg.

Thanks to everyone at FC2, especially Dan Waterman, Brian Evenson, Susan Steinberg, and Brenda "Don't Need a That There" Mills for their editorial and production work.

And much gratitude for daily inspiration to Immanuel Kant, Bruce Springsteen, and Eileen Myles.

For Kate

Many frantic cruelties occur to the flesh of the imagination
And the imagination does have flesh to destroy
And the flesh has imagination to sever
The mouth is just a body filled with imagination
Can you imagine its contents
The dripping into a bucket

—Lyn Hejinian, "Elegy"

Hey somebody out there
Listen to my last prayer
Hiho Silver-o
Deliver me from nowhere

—Bruce Springsteen, "State Trooper"

If I had actually spent any part of that first night asleep, it is difficult for me to know now, though no more difficult than it was for me to know then. I had believed, I think, for a long time, and perhaps I still do, that I had not slept at all that first night of my final year. I had not dozed, or at least believed that I had not dozed, even a tiny bit, but only lay there in my bed, looking out into the darkness inside the four walls. It was not just the experience of an unfamiliar room that kept me from rest, though that was, of course, part of it. But I had had new dormitory rooms three times before, one at the start of each school year, so this experience, an unfamiliar room, a new bed, was, actually, not completely new, but, now, as I begin to write, it seems clear that there was something palpably different that night. The confusion was palpable even before it became definite, as if already as I prepared myself for bed something unfamiliar hovered inside the room. But the fact that I was not sleeping was nothing new, though maybe I had been sleeping, but, in any case, I thought I wasn't, and this thought, this feeling, too, was nothing new because each time I had ever tried to sleep the first night in a new dormitory room I had not been able to sleep well or sleep at all. It stands to reason, then, that on this particular night too, I could not sleep or, at least, could not sleep very well or very much.

It is this confusion that makes my fourth and final time in a new dormitory room different, because although on the three other first nights in a new dormitory room I had not slept well, I had at least known that I had slept, not well, but I had slept. There was no doubt in my mind that I had slept, that I had each time, one way or another, no matter my mood or the circumstances surrounding the start of a new semester, fallen asleep. But this last time I had not known, am still not sure, if I had actually been sleeping, though it seems that I must have been. Or, maybe it's possible that I only thought the entire night that I was not asleep, but actually I was asleep and was only dreaming that I was awake, dreaming that I was staring out into the blank space of the dark room, watching my own thoughts make shadows on the wall until I felt her in bed next to me, breathing against my neck. And then I was too frightened to think my own thoughts. That's what I believe happened: though I thought that I was awake, thought that I was not asleep, I had, in actuality, I think, at least part of the time, been asleep, and in my sleep she visited me. She must have visited me. She must have been the dream. But you see, I could not know as I slept that I was actually sleeping because as I slept, I dreamt that I was awake. I dreamt that I was awake and that I was not alone in the room: she had finally come to visit me.

The TRANSLATION

I lived in an attic room of one of the older dormitories on the side of campus that used to house the women's college before the university turned coed. My room was small but had a large closet in which I was able to fit the dresser that came with the room without blocking my access to the hanging rod. The day that I moved into the room I placed the dresser flush against the back wall of the closet so that if I opened the closet door I stood directly in front of it with its drawers opening directly towards me and its left side flush against the left wall of the closet.

The closet was deep enough that I could still take one step into it and turn right. And it was wide enough for me to still walk three paces to the right of the dresser before getting to the hanging rod that hung perpendicular to the face of the dresser. On top of the dresser I kept my soap shampoo toothpaste toothbrush and washrag in a small plastic bucket unless I had just come out of the shower and then I would not keep the soap in the bucket but rather on top of a lid from an old margarine container until it dried. I kept the margarine lid on top of the dresser as well exactly next to the bucket so that the front edge of the lid and the front edge of the bucket were equidistant from the front edge of the dresser and when the washrag was wet after a shower I draped it neatly around the perimeter of the bucket so that it hung parallel to the bottom edge of the bucket until it dried too.

The bucket was white so I was careful to purchase only white cakes of soap white washrags a white toothbrush white tubes of toothpaste and shampoo that came in white bottles. Occasionally though my scalp would begin to itch and its skin would flake and for this reason I was forced to purchase a tar shampoo that had an amber color and came in a clear plastic bottle. In order not to disturb the arrangement of white that I kept neatly on top of the dresser which was oak I kept the tar shampoo in my sock drawer the top drawer of my dresser which was a fine decision since most of my socks were dark colored browns or blacks or grays. It was a better choice than for instance keeping the shampoo in the middle drawer with my underwear and bras which were white or in the bottom drawer with my T-shirts which were all white and my pajamas which were all blue. Besides I held the belief that things needn't be too orderly once in a drawer. In any case the difference in tone between the oak dresser itself and the objects on top of it made a subtle but pleasant contrast and the brightness of both kept the arrangement from appearing heavy and depressing and so I could be sure that its appearance would not affect my mood negatively when I woke in the mornings and was forced to open the closet door in order to prepare for my shower.

When I had finished arranging the closet I was pleased by the results and I only regretted that the closet was not big enough to hold my bed so that all items related to the care of my body could be neatly hidden from sight there behind the closed door since they were only needed late at night or early in the morning and it seemed strange for them to take up such a large portion of my living space. Had the closet been larger I could have slept in there keeping the closet door open at night so that fresh air or heat could enter depending on the season of course. Then in the mornings I could wake and wash and close the door on everything to do with my body and use the entirety of the room for those things that related to my studies specifically my bookshelves my books and my desk.

I had become very interested in the first stanza of the first poem of Rilke's *Duino Elegies* the entirety of which I was supposed to read for my German literature course but since my German was fairly poor I could only plod my way through the text by rendering a tedious translation for myself which required much dictionary work. Only then could I begin to grasp fully the poem whose first line had so absorbed me.

By about 1:00 a.m. on the first night that I began working on the poem I had sketched the first stanza for myself in English. I had printed a clean version of it by hand onto a piece of loose-leaf paper so that it would be easier to read than the working version in my notebook. Because I was tired from leaning over the dictionary for most of the evening I took the piece of paper and instead of sitting in my reading chair I lay down on my back on the bed. Since I am not in the habit of doing so I can only think now that I must have been extremely tired. And there I began to read the lines I had written:

Who if I cried out would hear me among the order of angels?
And even if one of them pressed me suddenly to his heart
Would I not die in his stronger being? For beauty is nothing
But the beginning of terror which we just barely endure.
Yet we admire it as it calmly refrains from destroying us.
Every Angel is terrifying.

It is clear to me now that it was the cry in the first line that appealed to me—that sound that would break the sealed capsule of a day as if there were something in me that could move beyond me. I thought about the sound for quite a while and concluded that it could not be a name. It could never be a word of any sort but only a sound. An unplanned unknown sound. Something the body could make independent of the mind's idea of it. A bellow. A marker of one's space loud and certain of its own uncertainty outside itself. There was nothing in me strong enough to make a sound like that.

But I knew where it would come from if it could come. I unbuttoned my pants and I pulled my shirt out and lifted it up so I could see myself. And I took my finger and made circles on my stomach dipping just under my navel and staying just inside the ribs. I made these circles slowly. That was the loudest call I could bear to make.

And when I began to feel the angel pressing on top of me—when I knew she had come I kept calling not with my fingers but only through my breath moving in and out of my mouth beneath her ear. She pulled me closer into her and for a moment I thought she was beautiful and I did not open my eyes but I imagined a face for her and the face I imagined wasn't unusual. It was the face of any girl and to make it angelic I gave her long curls and these fell upon me and I felt calm beneath her and I let her touch me and I let us be lost in one another. I didn't want to open my eyes to see her so I clasped her face with my hands and felt its form soft in my palms. It felt just as I had wanted it to feel and I pulled it close against my own. I could feel the heat from the streak of red across her cheek. It became too hot against my face so I pushed away. I felt cool again for a moment but then her body grew warm around me and she began to move faster against me and her heat gradually took me over and except for my face and thoughts I could not tell the feeling of myself from the feeling of her.

But soon I had the urge to open my eyes and I did but I couldn't see her face only her hair and I felt suddenly where my body ended and where hers began and so I felt nervous. I couldn't move my neck because she was so close on top of me but I strained my eyes downwards and when I did I saw her swollen breasts crushing my own and I could see the small hairs on them and I thought of hog flesh as the tops of them grazed my neck and the underside of my chin as I struggled to break free. She had grown so heavy that it was impossible to pull away from her. I could only feel her hairy swine breasts pricking my skin and her body pushing the breath out of me. Her wings flapped rapidly up and down thrusting her hips hard against mine. I felt the springs of the mattress pressing painfully into me from underneath.

Her wings were white but filthy like a pigeon's and longer than the length of me. They closed upon us making a cave for me beneath her. And their smell surrounded me: an unwashed dog. She grunted in pain each time they came down because her left wing had no room to fall along the right side of me but would bend and scrape against the wall and sound like a branch swiping across the side of a house in a storm but here it was incessant like a heartbeat and since the wings came so quickly the grunts were rapid too. They became louder and louder as if they were coming from deeper inside of her and she didn't stop but pushed her wings with greater force as if she were testing her own strength. It became more difficult to rise with her since she was pushing me with every round deeper down into the mattress. I was sweating now and had no more breath in me and then with the strength of terror that the helplessness gathered I rose again and gasped and heaved and quickly shook my head. I had wished her away.

When I entered the women's shower room the light was turned off as it usually was when I entered to shower but this time I was entering to shower at night which I never did and because I never turned the light on when I entered to shower I had to consider carefully what I was going to do now. I only had to think for a moment about whether to turn the lights on and then I saw that the streetlights surrounding the parking lot out back were sending an orange glow into the bathroom that reflected off the white tiles and the chrome and the mirrors that lined the walls across from the showers. Mornings I always opened the window twelve inches before showering so I thought that if I did this now more light would flood the room and there would be no reason for me to break my habit now and turn the light switch on despite the hour. I walked to the shower stall as I always did and opened the curtain. I placed my bucket in the right-hand corner furthest from the showerhead and then hung my towel on the hook outside the stall.

At the window I could see the wind was blowing hard and the streetlights made a shadow of a tree branch dance across the frosted glass in front of me. When I opened it the light and shadow fell flat off the glass onto my body and the light and shadow that didn't fit onto my body fell off my hips and stretched out onto the floor. Limbs moved on my stomach and if I looked down on myself to see where they fell I could feel a slight pressure through my robe—a warmth as if I were being touched but of course I wasn't being touched but seeing the shadows of the branches there made me feel as though I were being touched. As long as I looked it was as though I were being touched and so I felt touched.

In the shower I could hear the branches etching against the glass behind the sound of water. If it weren't for the sound of them there was nothing I could have seen that would have made me think that there was anyone outside the curtain and I would have just showered in the dark. But the scratching on the glass made me think I wasn't alone and sometimes I would stick my head out of the curtain to see if I were alone and I would see myself alone in the mirror looking at the light and shadows. It's difficult to say why I felt I wouldn't be alone but there was something about the way the branch moved that made me think of a girl dancing outside the curtain and when I opened the curtain and stepped out to dry myself the light and shadows were there again and in the mirror I could see I was in the shadows and I knew when I saw her there that she wouldn't ever leave me and I was scared though I wasn't in the dark anymore. I was standing in the light now too.

It's difficult to say how I brought her here or how she had fallen into the mirror because when I turned around to look in the stall she wasn't standing behind me but was just there in front of me in the mirror. She was trapped in the glass though in my bed she had been able to fall on me in sleep. Poems make it easy to dream of angels but the girl she had no wings so she couldn't have been the angel. I thought that I knew that I didn't know her so I thought it best not to move. And even though she was someone very much like me still she was strange and I was scared and I couldn't have been just looking at myself and been so scared. And then I moved closer to the mirror because I wanted to make sure she wasn't me. And she followed me to the mirror so I thought for a second I was right. She was me and I didn't have to be scared and I moved my eyes to the right and then to the left and she did the same but then I thought I saw her lip curl about to smile but I was too nervous to smile so I knew that she wasn't me. She was some stranger come to trick me and in the second that I thought she wasn't me she felt too close. She was too close to me and I was scared she would creep inside me and before I even thought what to do I swung. I swung and I wanted to hit her but I hadn't hit her. I didn't hit her and I fell. I had fallen. I fell against the mirror and she was gone. And then my head began to pulse where it had hit the glass so I put my nose to the mirror and watched the blood push there to make the skin swell. The skin above my eye rose and stretched. A darkening bruise swallowed it.

Something shone in the light and where it shone I felt a sharp pain and when I pushed it it was hard and it cut into my finger. I pushed the bruise from the side to squeeze the glass out like the puss of a pimple and when it came out my head bled a little.

When I saw the blood I hoped that I wouldn't vomit but whenever I see my own blood I vomit and I was sure now that it was my own blood and it was because I touched it. And I was sure that it was my own body getting sick because I saw myself buckle over in the mirror. I couldn't see myself get ill because my head was down but I could see the floor and I could see what came out of me onto the floor and I could feel what came out of me and when I was done having everything come out of me I looked in the mirror and saw that my lip was still dirty so I knew it was me who was ill. And then Amanda came into the bathroom by chance and turned the lights on just after I finished being ill and suddenly the shadows and the branches were gone and I was just standing there under the fluorescent lights in my plastic shoes next to my own vomit with my head bleeding and a piece of the mirror missing. I couldn't tell her what happened because it was hard for me to explain my imagination especially on a night when my head was bleeding and there was a piece of the mirror missing.

I told her I had gotten dizzy because I ate something bad and then the heat of the shower made me feel worse so I got out and was going to go to my room to lie down but before I could leave the shower room I fell and vomited there right outside the shower in front of the mirror because I was so weak and I asked her if she thought the bruise was bad and she said *No M—. It doesn't look too bad. It will probably go away in a few days.* But it didn't.

The HAM STEAK

I sat and ate my ham where I sat every night and ate my ham or my roast beef or my chicken or my turkey or whatever other meat was due to be served according to the plan of food services. I sat at the head of a long dark brown wooden table that was near the center of the east dining room and I sat there as I did every night with my friends who were amused by my habits and I didn't mind that they were amused and I was grateful to have friends to eat with because otherwise I would be simply eating the ham by myself. Although I could not let myself stop seeing the beauty in the way that I ate ham I was grateful not to be alone when eating ham because the sense of pleasure that I felt when I ate it as I wished to eat it seemed so great that I was often scared to be lost in the detail of my experience thereby losing the sense of my greater surroundings.

The ham in the dining hall was cut by machine into steaks that were about a quarter of an inch thick and they were a light pink but there was an iridescent purple film that shone on the flesh. When it was put on an institutional white plate and handed to me by the men working in the dining hall who wore white caps and white shirts it was handed to me almost sideways. The plate was never completely parallel to the ground. Maybe it was almost nearly parallel to the ground but I was careful to notice each time they handed me a plate of ham that because of the way the human hand is built it was easier for the server to hand me my plate of ham in the cafeteria line in such a way that the side of the plate bent slightly in the direction that his thumb pointed. If it were being served by a right-handed person for example who of course held it from the side closest to him with the thumb coming over the lip of the plate it was easiest for him to hand it to me so that the plate was slightly bent in a direction towards his feet and the center of his body. The plate was handed to me at an angle that pointed down somewhere between the left and the right arm not somewhere in a direction outside to the right or left of the body. Because of the angle at which the ham steak was handed to me because it was at an angle not parallel to the ceiling my eye would catch the meat in the fluorescent light in a certain way that let me see that the ham steak that I was about to eat was not pink but that it was covered in a purple film an iridescent purple film like the inside of a sea shell. This made me think that the meat had a special kind of magic. It wasn't an extraordinary magic but an ordinary one. It was the magic of knowing that the comforting order of the ordinary which sometimes appeared as the extraordinary purple glow of a piece of meat was in fact just ordinary and it would always rise to greet my mind in the exact same manner that it had greeted it before and for this reason I loved to eat ham steak best.

I liked my ham served with a light brown gravy. I liked it served with peas and mashed potatoes. I have always liked it this way although I can't recall if I have always liked it this way because it was the way it had always been served at school and I liked anything that had always been done a certain way so I grew to love ham dinners because they were always done the same way at school. Or else I had liked to eat ham dinners this way before I arrived at school and school had always served it to me the way I liked so I could trust that school was a place where things would be done always in the same way to please me and things wouldn't change in ways to surprise me but dinners would always go on and on the same way forever so there would be nothing new to look forward to and there would always be ham to feed me.

And this evening was no different from any other evening. Because it was no different from any other evening ham was served it was possible for me to ignore the bruise on my forehead and to forget that the evening before this one had been different from any other evening. But this evening just as I would have done on any other evening that ham was served I arranged my plate into equal thirds with three triangles intersecting at the center of the plate.

The ham steak was in the bottom triangle closest to me on the table and the potatoes were in the top left triangle on the plate and the peas in the top right triangle of the plate. I poured gravy over all three food items to act as a kind of unifying force. I ate European style as my mother had taught: with the knife in my right hand and my fork in my left hand. The two worked simultaneously and I never put one implement down without putting down the other. The fork was in my left hand with its bubbled back facing towards the ceiling. I pushed its teeth into the edge of the ham steak and cut it with my knife so that a piece of meat extended forward from the teeth of the fork. This I used as a ledge onto which I would next push a bit of the mashed potatoes with my knife and on top of the potatoes which now rose in a mound off the back of my fork I would then push a number of peas that would stay on the back of the fork due to the stickiness of the potatoes and the gravy. Then I would lift the fork into my mouth and have a perfect medley of all the flavors present on my plate. I chewed rather quickly mostly due to my hunger but partially due to my anxiety about chewing the ham in such a way that would cause my teeth to slip against one another and make a disturbing squeaky noise in my mouth that made me jump suddenly in my chair. In any case I was able to avoid this feeling that night and was also able to divide my portions up in such a way that I ran out of all food items simultaneously and despite a general feeling of nervousness I was not forced to eat the ham alone or the ham with just potatoes or the ham with just peas or just the peas with the potatoes or the peas alone or the potatoes alone.

As I ate my friends sat around me in their usual arrangement and I had a way of being with them that gave them the feeling that we were really close friends and I did this by raising my head in between bites of food and looking at them and smiling as they told me their stories. Despite this however there were certain things I would not tell my friends because I was a very private person and I wanted to remain private. I wanted to protect my imagination because my imagination was the means by which I made myself into a writer and there was nothing more important to me than being a writer. Though sometimes there were things that could not remain private by nature for instance the bruise on my forehead with the cut from the tiny piece of glass from the mirror I had fallen into the night before. But I could not betray the story of the bruise because if I gave up the story of the bruise then I would be giving up the story of my imagination and my imagination was the only means by which I could be myself and I needed to be myself to begin writing because my own story seemed to be the only story I could tell.

But in the writing once I started to write the story of myself she seemed to become another body and she would sometimes for instance if I were to give her the bruise which I gave myself the night before she would sometimes not carry the bruise well. She would sometimes take what I had given her and make it into something else and suddenly the bruise that I had given myself in the bathroom the night before would in the writing become a gash in the leg and there would suddenly be a girl there with a gash in her leg and I would be confused and begin to doubt that there was ever really a bruise on my forehead and perhaps now I should begin limping to the dining hall because in the writing I was denied the privilege of being myself and most of all I wanted to be myself. But when I sat there alone at night with a pen in my hand trying to write myself and suddenly there was this other with my face and a gash in her leg I could only get up from the desk and limp.

She never seemed to have much sympathy for me and I knew this because she could never for instance just take my bruise and the point of the writing to begin with was to have another self that would take the bruise so I wouldn't have to walk around limping so that my friends wouldn't have to ask me questions and I wouldn't have to betray the story of my imagination and how it sometimes landed on my forehead but never really seemed able to land in my writing. But I had read that semester in a book by Maurice Blanchot who had written about Franz Kafka that that was the problem with writing. No matter how hard Jozef K tried to be Franz Kafka in the book it was still Jozef K standing at a window with his papers waiting for a clerk and not Franz Kafka sitting at a desk with a pen in his hand. And so no matter how hard someone tried to write herself into a book at night there could never be the self in a book that had sympathy for the self that was writing and this made the writing both impossible and endless and though it was difficult for me I was forced to look for sympathy outside myself.

But even the stories I didn't write down betrayed me when I tried to tell them to someone. For instance it was clear that both my friends and I knew that I hadn't gotten the bruise because last night's dinner made me so ill that I fell and hit my head. They had eaten the same dinner so they and I both knew the bruise on my forehead with the cut from the tiny piece of glass from the mirror I had fallen into the night before did not arrive there on my forehead by the story I gave it. They knew that it arrived there by a story that refused to betray itself because it felt that it was my story and would not let me share it with anyone else. Given this fact I was forced to consider those people my friends who weren't particularly upset that the story I had made for the bruise wasn't the real story because the real story refused to be told. I had to consider those people my friends who would give me a bandage for my bruise and maybe a dab of antiseptic and a bit of sympathy while at the same time pretending to believe a story that they knew wasn't true.

And so on this particular evening during which I ate my ham steak with a fresh bruise on my forehead my friends just looked at me while I ate my ham steak and if they did ask me about the bruise on my forehead they believed the story that I told them. They believed that I had eaten a dinner that had upset my stomach and maybe it was difficult for them to believe this because they too had eaten the turkey the night before yet they were all sitting here now at the dinner table without any bruises on their foreheads or even gashes in their legs although I couldn't expect any of them to have gashes in their legs because none of them were writers but yet none of them had bruises on their foreheads and so it was obvious to all of us that the reason I had a bruise on my forehead was because I was not telling them the story of my imagination and for some reason this made me feel distant from them and close to them at the same time.

G—

That night I felt lonely at dinner because of the bruise on my forehead so when I finished my dessert I didn't return to my room but went to find G— who was neither a friend nor a story I had ever told to anyone and I wanted to find her because I knew I could be with her any way I chose because she didn't know my friends and when I left her room she would just disappear and I wouldn't have to explain anything to anyone. I could just sleep with her.

What I liked about being with G— was that her lights were always on low and she never had much to say to me and although I didn't feel very comfortable when we were in bed together at least I didn't have to talk although sometimes when we were naked and the room was dark I had the strange need to try to talk to her and I would tell her she was beautiful not because I necessarily felt that she was beautiful—it was too dark to see that she was beautiful—but because I thought that if I said something nice to her she would maybe ask me how my bruise was doing but she would never say anything back and when she didn't say anything back I knew that I had forgotten that she was someone who wasn't really in my life but that she was only a breathing body beneath me who knew nothing about the dining hall or my bruise or my imagination or how I would fall into mirrors at night and she never said anything that made me think she wanted to know anything about me or my imagination and that is why I thought maybe we could love each other.

When I came into her room that night she didn't say anything about the bruise on my forehead which is why I came to see her that night so when she didn't say anything I knew that everything would be all right and maybe she did now really want to love me and I should just continue on in the manner that I always did. I didn't really feel like touching her right then when I came in the door but I knew that I needed to touch her if I wanted her to let me stay so I touched her. And although each time I touched her I didn't want to at first once I did I kept wanting to touch her and that was because she felt soft and though I didn't want to touch her because something in me always felt a little ill when I touched someone I kept touching her because her lips and her neck were soft enough that when I touched her I felt as much good as I felt bad. But I never let her touch me back and she didn't seem to really want to so we had a way of being with each other where both of us understood the rules and so we were able to take our clothes off together the same way each time.

That is first I kissed her and I kissed her until she started to breathe heavy. When I heard her breathing heavy I put my hand against her breast and then when she sighed after I put my hand on her breast I knew I could push her to the bed and once she was on the bed and stopped me from kissing her anymore and smiled I knew she wanted me to take off her shirt so I would take off her shirt and then she would run her fingers on the back of my head and that's when I knew that she wanted me to kiss her breasts and suck on her nipples. If while I was kissing her breasts and sucking on her nipples she still rubbed the back of my head I knew to put my hand between her legs to see if through her jeans I could feel she was getting wet. If I felt a heat there and she began tugging at my earlobe while I felt the heat there I knew it was ok to keep my hand in between her legs and press and if I ever felt excited it was usually at this time and I didn't like it if I felt excited because then I felt slightly dizzy and it was hard for me to keep thinking if she was getting wetter there between her legs where I was pressing and it became hard to pay attention to her pulling on my ear and I didn't want to miss any of her signals so if I got excited while my hand was in between her legs I would begin reciting poems that I memorized in high school and so I was able to keep count of her ear tugs and keep my hand pressing in an even way against her just as long as I could keep saying to myself *Whose woods these are I think I know* and as long as I could keep reciting the poem in my head I could keep my body under control and get G—'s pants off of her so I could continue pleasing her.

This time I did get very excited and I was chanting the poem to myself and shaking my head back and forth so that I could shake my body out of my thoughts and just keep the poem there but it was getting harder and harder and I could feel myself swelling in my pants and I got so feverish that I let go of the poem and pulled G—'s pants off and just as I moved my face in between her legs just as I was about to lick her thighs I saw three cuts there three cuts that I hadn't seen before on her thighs but only on her wrists and now they were here on her thighs and suddenly the poem came back in my head and I stopped and sat up.

Had I been anyone else or had G— been anyone else the fact that I suddenly sat up in bed the fact that I was moving my head out from between her legs would not have been dramatic but as I sat up I knew I was breaking our rules and our rules were not made to be broken and I knew that it was not possible for either of us to have been anyone else and to be here together but breaking our rules made it appear as though I had become someone else and for this reason I knew that it was not possible for me to move my head out from between her legs at this moment but because I was doing it meant now suddenly that things would be different between us and what that difference would be I was not sure but I knew that it made me nervous so I tried to behave in a way that made the difference not seem so great.

G—'s head jerked up nervously and her eyes came wide open as her arms spread out behind her to hold her body up above her pillow. This is how she asked me for an explanation and although I knew I had done something bad I thought my only way of salvaging the situation was to act as if I didn't know that I had done something bad so I said *I just wanted to stop to look at how beautiful you are.* I knew the sentence would confuse her because suddenly I was not myself but myself pretending to be someone's lover a lover who I could never be and had no way of being because I was incapable of uttering the sentence *I just wanted to stop to look at how beautiful you are* without pretending to be someone else and that fact made me someone who could never sleep with someone who needed their lover to utter that sentence sincerely and the fact that I pretended to utter the sentence sincerely also made me someone who could never sleep with G—.

These thoughts were streaming through my head as I uttered the sentence and I knew suddenly that I had to stop thinking if I were to make my lie believable because someone who was able to say the sentence I just said would not be someone who could think but someone who could feel. In an effort to be someone who wasn't thinking which I knew when I started was an impossible task I began rubbing G—'s leg and for a second I did stop thinking and the second in which I wasn't thinking was the first second I touched her thigh and the skin was soft—soft enough to excite me and make me not think of anything except my own body swelling—but the not thinking felt so good that it made me move my hand and suddenly I felt the lip of the cut skin on her leg and then my thinking started again and I kept thinking that my finger was falling into her cut and moving around in the flesh and blood and I couldn't stop it and these thoughts made my face burn.

In my head I imagined that my finger was deep in her cut hurting her but on her thigh my hand was now running over her cuts and in between her legs because I didn't want G— to know what I was thinking now and when I reached the lips between her legs they were wet and I looked down now to make sure they weren't the cut but only the place where I usually stuck my fingers and where G— usually liked it. It was so I put my fingers in there but in my head I thought that my fingers were still in the cut on her thigh and although I knew this wasn't true I couldn't help thinking that it was and each time I looked at G— it was easy to think that it was both true and not true because her eyes were closed and she kept turning her head slowly back and forth grunting *Oh Oh Oh* and so she only helped the thinking to keep going.

I kept trying to change the thoughts because I thought that if I couldn't stop them then I should try to change them. So every time in my thoughts I thought I was putting my finger in G—'s wound I thought instead that she was Jesus and I was doubting Thomas and that by putting my fingers in her wound I was saving myself and this thought would make me push my fingers deeper inside of her and it would make her groan louder but each time she groaned louder I got scared that I was hurting her and then I began thinking again that I wasn't doubting Thomas and she wasn't Jesus and I was just sticking my finger in the cut in her thigh and I was just hurting her. And when I began to think that I was hurting her my face would begin to burn and my heart would beat faster and I would sweat and I couldn't take this feeling so then I would imagine that I was tying my hands up in the branches that I saw in the mirror the night I got the bruise and once my hands were tied up I imagined another me pushing my head into the mirror every time I heard G— groan and because I had the bruise on my forehead to prove it I knew that that thought was true and that instead of hurting G— I was just hurting myself and that made me feel better and I kept thinking this until she came and I felt good afterwards because I didn't hurt her and I thought that I made her feel good.

But my good feeling didn't last long because G— knew that I had put my fingers in her cut and I knew that she knew this because after she finished coming she sat up in bed without looking at me and she got out of bed without looking at me and she went into a dark corner of the room and sat in that dark corner naked with her knees folded up to her shoulders like upside down Vs and she sat there smoking and I could see her face light up around the cigarette for a second as she lit the match and her eyes were big and her face was beautiful with long hollow cheeks and big red lips just as I had imagined it so I knew that everything I thought was true because it all flashed true even with the slightest bit of light.

Her eyes didn't look at me and this is how I knew that something was wrong and because I had been putting my fingers in her cuts I knew that I was the something that was wrong. And because she didn't stay in bed and because she didn't smile at me after coming I knew that what I did that was wrong hurt her and there was nothing that I could do about it and because she didn't talk and because she didn't look at me and because things were different now than they usually were after G— came I had to figure out a new way for us to be. There seemed no way now to go back to our rules because they were broken now and although most things that were broken could usually be fixed like for instance a window there were certain things in the world that once they were broken couldn't be fixed and because they couldn't be fixed then they just became something else like for instance a virgin and so I knew that what I broke in G— couldn't be fixed and now she was something else so all I could do was put my clothes on and tell her I was sorry and kiss her cold face and walk out the door and that was the last time I ever slept with G—.

That night I dreamt that G— was walking towards me with cuts on the insides of her arms. She was coming towards me with open arms showing me the cuts that she had just made on the insides of her arms and in the dream she spoke to me although in real life she hardly ever spoke to me and in the dream she said to me *You did this to me* and in the dream I said back to her over and over again *I didn't do that to you* but she in the dream always spoke back to me *Yes you did this to me* and this went on in the dream for what seemed like a very long time until in the dream I got very angry and finally said *Yes I did this to you* and then I took a knife and cut her arms over and over again and I kept saying *Yes I'm doing this to you* and it felt good to say that in the dream because I no longer had to worry that I had done something wrong because I was doing something wrong and doing something wrong felt better than worrying about doing something wrong and it felt so good to cut her in the dream because I no longer had to worry that I might cut her and when it started to feel good I woke up because even in the dream I was worried that bad things made me feel good.

The next morning I saw G— on campus and she stopped and spoke to me and when she spoke to me she smiled and so I didn't mind speaking to her and we spoke for quite a long time but then I saw new cuts on her arms and I thought *I did that to her.*

The BRIDGE

If a person stood on campus facing east she could see beyond the towering Sciences Library a rusty iron bridge on the horizon open and erect over the Seekonk River. If a person stood on the road that ran along the river she could see that the bridge was preceded by a field of tall grasses that grew to the very edge of the river and seemed to grow to the very mouth of the bridge though there must have been a road that led on to the bridge or had once led on to the bridge but I had never walked that far out to the bridge but only once stood in the grasses in front of it.

Only once had I walked to the bridge. Once when I first came to school and knew nothing about the bridge I walked to the bridge early in the morning because I couldn't sleep.

I headed east towards the bridge because I could see the bridge clearer than anything else. And following the sight of the bridge I walked past the Portuguese bakery and past the wooden houses of Fox Point over the Little League field into the grasses where I stopped and stood though I hadn't quite reached the bridge and I watched the early sunlight filter through the rusty girders of the old bridge until the light of the horizon became so bright that I had to turn away.

There were many stories about the bridge and many stories about the places around the bridge and often when people wanted to be alone they walked towards the bridge and stood in the grasses staring at the bridge and the water and the sun. And once in the dining hall Nate told me that if I had gone just a little bit north of the bridge just a little bit beyond the Little League field I would have come to a stretch of road along the river that was cut off from sight of any houses. A stretch of road that was flanked on one side by the river and its grasses and on the other side by woods. Nate said if I had just walked north along the river I would have come to this road and along this road by the river I would have found a string of cars parked not all in a row one in front of the other but a short distance from one another and if I came to this stretch of road and saw these cars he said I would see in many of these cars a man sitting alone at the wheel and I would wonder why so many men were sitting in cars alone along the river but then Nate said possibly if I waited long enough I would see one of the men maybe get out of his car and walk over to another car and get into the car with another man. Or I would see two men walking across the road into the woods together. And he said that he knew a boy from school who had walked down to that part of the river and had gotten into a car with one of those men. And the man told the boy that if his wife was only willing to do to him what the boy was willing to do to him along the river he wouldn't have to come and park down by the river. And though I still thought the bridge was beautiful after I heard the story from Nate I never went back to the river and each time I looked east from campus and saw the bridge erect in the sky even though I still thought it was beautiful for some reason the sight of the bridge despite the fact that it was still beautiful made me feel very lonely.

A SPLINTER in the BELLY

In writing workshop my professor would often not say anything about the student's story that we were discussing for a very long time and then he would let out a large sigh and with his pointer finger push up his glasses and then run his hands through his hair and then he would say for example *Now Daniel you have the potential to be a writer to be a very good writer but by writing a novel about a writer who writes boring novels that put everyone asleep you are doing nothing except writing a boring novel in which nothing happens and your readers are put to sleep and how are you going to become a writer if all your readers are asleep*? I could see the professor's point but I liked Daniel very much because he had the ability to be the smartest person in the class without ever really saying very much and he had a big head of red curly hair and even though he didn't ever say very much he had already for seven years been compulsively transcribing everything he heard or read along with everything he said or thought into a kind of sign language that he had invented (technically a binary hand-alphabet that looked more or less like fidgeting or piano playing). Daniel told me once that he noticed that even when there wasn't anything to transcribe into the hand-alphabet he would find his hand repeating the phrase *We have no choice—We have no choice* and when he told me about that I got very nervous because I knew that Daniel was smarter than I was and I was worried that his hands were even smarter than he was and maybe then it was true we had no choice and I didn't want that to be true because more than anything I wanted to think that the world was the way it was because I didn't want it to change but not because it couldn't change. I wanted to live in a world that could change if I wanted it to change though I didn't think that I wanted it to change but I wanted it to be able to change in case I ever thought I wanted it to change and while the professor was saying these things about Daniel's novel Daniel's hands tapped quickly against one another and I could tell Daniel was getting ready to argue with the professor and I was right because as soon as the professor finished Daniel said *The novel does at least pretend to be an ordinary novel. It preserves the conventions of the novel—the speakers are individualized characters in an identifiable situation. This means that at any moment the characters might stop talking and start doing something. Of course they won't but this option is always available to them.* And the only thing the professor said to Daniel after that was *Possibility is not the same as fact* and then the room fell silent and I could see Daniel's hands moving quickly and I knew he was shouting *We have no choice—We have no choice* but no one except me could hear him. And I could only wonder then if his characters really had a choice because it was impossible to know if Daniel's hands were smarter than his mouth and even though what Daniel said to the professor made me think that Daniel was maybe smarter than the professor still I couldn't argue that possibility was the same as fact. It wasn't. Being able to change and changing were two different things.

And then we moved on to L— who had written a story about a woman lying in a bathtub dreaming about having a baby. And in the dream the baby was born with a wooden leg and I thought this was a great story because I liked thinking about a baby born with a wooden leg because I liked trying to think about how a piece of wood could attach itself to a baby who never had yet been in the world to see a piece of wood and I liked thinking about it because even though I could imagine many different ways for it to happen none of the things I imagined seemed right so the story just kept me thinking forever hoping I would find the right answer but of course there was no right answer but still trying to find the right answer made me feel smart because I could watch myself think so I thought for a long time about how the wood could get into the womb of the woman but I couldn't think of a way and so I just kept thinking and if there was anything I learned at school it was that there was nothing I liked more than thinking about questions that had no answers because then I could just go on thinking forever and there was nothing I enjoyed more than feeling myself think but when I told this to my professor he said *Yes of course M— everyone likes to feel himself think but you are wrong when you say there is a baby born with a wooden leg in L—'s piece. There is in the piece only the dream of a baby being born with a wooden leg and for that reason* he said *there might as well have been no baby born with a wooden leg in this piece and there is no reason for you to think about how a baby could be born with a wooden leg after reading this piece because anything can happen in a dream and this dream in particular has no effect on a real world because in this story after the woman wakes up from dreaming in a bathtub about giving birth to a baby with a wooden leg she only gets up from the tub and dries her body and for that reason there might as well be no dream and no baby with a wooden leg.* And then he stopped to sigh and fix his glasses and run his hands through his hair and then he started up again and I hoped he wouldn't talk about what I said anymore because I realized suddenly that what I said about thinking was stupid and I shouldn't have thought so much after reading something that was just a dream. Luckily he only talked about L— now and he said if L— wanted the dream of the child born with a wooden leg to actually be something that happened in her story there had to be a consequence to the dream. The woman in the story would have to do something else besides dry herself with a towel. She would have to for instance wake from the dream and find a splinter in her belly. Or if L— didn't like the idea of putting a splinter in the belly he said she could just make her give birth to a child with a wooden leg. He said she could just forget the dream because it was a story and anything could happen in a story as long as something happened—even a child born with a wooden leg. But I didn't understand this because I always felt having dreamt many dreams that there was always a lot happening in dreams and why couldn't a dream also be something happening? But I didn't say anything because I didn't want to feel stupid again. But L— said she didn't like the professor's answer because she didn't think it was real for a child to be born with a wooden leg or even for a woman to find a splinter in her belly but that it was real for a woman to dream of giving birth to a child with a wooden leg because she did have a dream that she gave birth to a child with a wooden leg and all she did afterwards was get out of the bathtub and dry herself and L— didn't want anything that wasn't real in her stories but then the professor got mad at her and said *Well then why are you writing fiction if you don't want anything unreal in your stories* and I have to admit he had a point but I still couldn't stop thinking that dreams were real stories too with or without a splinter in the belly.

At the TABLE

The hanging lamp above the table shone out against the darkness outside the kitchen so that if someone had come up to the window my mother and father and I would not have seen her face but she could have stared at us furtively from the dew-covered grass of the dark yard as we sat there lit under the hanging lamp that hung above the kitchen table. At the table once the dishes were cleared my father began to tell us a story that night and even though I was very small—small enough to feel protected while sitting at the table between my mother and father—as my father told the story I couldn't help both to listen to the story and as I was listening to the story also to think that there was someone at the window in the darkness watching me listen to the story and thinking that there was someone at the window watching me listen to the story had the strange effect of making me imagine myself listening to the story as I sat there and listened to the story. And maybe my father sensed her at the window too because for some reason on this particular night he told us a story that he hadn't ever told us before. He told us the story of something that happened to him when he was not much bigger than I was on this night that I was both listening to him tell the story and watching myself listen to him tell the story at the kitchen table.

What my father said that night was that when he was a small boy big enough to know how to swim but not big enough to swim in the river by himself he was sent to the river with an aunt who was to watch him swim. But when my father was swimming in the river his aunt who was sent to watch him swim began to read and didn't notice when he was pulled under water by the current of the river that came whirling around him. While the aunt who was sent by my father's parents to protect him from drowning lay in the grass along the river lost in the sentences of her book his small body was sucked under water so quickly that in a matter of a few seconds he lay at the bottom of the river exactly as if his small body had been put to sleep in a real bed. And as he lay there almost sleeping at the bottom of the river that never should have been like a real bed his ghost rose out of him like a ghost rises out of any person when he is a small boy about to drown at the bottom of the river and there is no one there to save him. But instead of leaving his body at the bottom of the river and taking his spirit somewhere else his ghost floated out of him and hovered above him and watched his body struggle not to sleep at the bottom of the river and because his ghost rose out of him but did not leave him and instead floated above him and watched him his ghost could see what the boy needed to do to save his body. The ghost could see exactly what rock the boy's legs needed to push off from so that he could propel his body head first through the surface of the water and rise into air and breathe again. Because the spirit no longer was inside the body of the boy the spirit could help the body of the boy save itself because the spirit could watch the body when no one else did and it was the spirit that told the body to push off that rock with the last of its strength and break through the surface of the river and it did break through with its mouth wide open sucking in air at last though no one else except the ghost had been able to watch the body and save it from drowning. And when he came out of the water where he had almost drowned he didn't say a word to his aunt when she turned to smile at him. He just sat down next to her and let the sun dry the mud off his back.

And even though his ghost had been able to save him from not drowning the story made me think from the moment that I heard it that my father by fathering me had made me a person in his own likeness and though my father had only lived a few seconds with his ghost outside of his body my body seemed to move in the world watched by its own ghost always as if its ghost had never yet come inside it and was always waiting to one day be a part of me so that I could finally become myself. And though I believed that the way I was forced to live with my ghost outside of my body was the result of being my father's daughter the more I thought about it the more I could not deny that my father's ghost had left him only for a few seconds to save him from death but my ghost hovered next to me for years with the hope of one day coming inside my body so that I could finally be born into life. And I could tell that my ghost was eager to come inside my body because unlike my father's ghost my ghost didn't ever rise above me but floated just close enough alongside me so that I couldn't help but think of it as my own shadow hoping to slip inside me—the object that cast it.

My ghost followed me so closely that if for instance I moved my arm to grab an apple I had not only the feeling of the apple in my hand but also the feeling of watching someone's arm grab an apple so that I felt both that it was my arm grabbing the apple and not my arm grabbing the apple. Something that so clearly should have felt like my own experience seemed both to be my own experience and the experience of another person who I never was able to reach but always seemed able to watch. Even when I would see this strange hand press the apple into my mouth I could barely feel the mealy flesh on my tongue though I could very clearly see myself chewing the very apple I just saw a strange arm lift and push into my mouth and this made it seem as though the experience of eating the apple was not my own at all even though I had a piece of its skin stuck between my teeth.

And because I wandered around empty of my own spirit there was a way that my body needed to fill itself with something until it was ready to take in its own ghost and permit me to begin my life and become a real person. So my body filled itself up with all the words I read in books so that the passages that I read dwelled inside me as if they themselves had been my own acute memories of actual lived experiences and although at the time it wasn't clear to me why it was the words I read in books that something inside me chose as a substitute for its own ghost it seems to me now that maybe just as my father's ghost had seen a rock at the bottom of the river for his dying body to push off from and save itself my ghost had sensed that each little passage of literature I read for school had its own spirit and that each time my body was able to swallow the body of a book it also ingested with it a complete spirit that was not separate from its letters. And so for this reason I believe that in some strange way my own ghost was trying to save me by forcing me to ingest these books that it hoped could show me how to live finally through example. The problem my ghost did not foresee was that even though each passage I memorized showed me how something that had a body could also have a spirit inside it in order for the words to teach me this lesson I had to let them fill up the empty space where my own spirit should have lived so that the books and parts of books that lived inside me both taught me what it would be like to live with my spirit inside me and left no room for my spirit itself. But it was difficult even for me to notice sometimes that my ghost didn't dwell inside me because despite the fact that I often felt like the quietest person at our table so many of the words that lived inside me would come out of my mouth that even though in hindsight I can't help but think that it was very apparent that these words I spoke were not my own words the passages that I had memorized were so spirited that both my friends and I were charmed by them enough to assume that the spirit of these words was also a part of my own spirit. So that while I was reciting some passage so fervently that the words themselves felt a part of my body and the whole table couldn't help but stop to listen to me both my friends and I were too intoxicated to notice that I was also standing alone outside the refectory with my nose pressed against the window watching both my friends and me forget I wasn't even there with them.

Because of this problem of not being ever truly inside myself I was attracted to things that seemed to be just themselves and nothing more and though there was almost nothing in the universe that didn't in its being refer to a world beyond itself I found that the sparrows around campus were nothing but themselves all day long and never seemed to question the fact that they really were sparrows and I could tell this by the look in their eyes as they were eating or searching for something to eat. Their look was so intent upon scouring the ground for a possible meal that I could not help but think that the sparrows believed fiercely in the fact that the ground they walked on existed and most importantly that they too existed because they walked intently upon the ground and thought little of it.

And ever since L— in writing class found it so difficult to imagine a possibility for her story that wasn't part of her own true story even though the professor had yelled at her for lacking imagination I couldn't help but become intrigued with her for refusing to write a story that didn't contain anything but what she knew to be her own true experience because I could not imagine ever being able to know if my own experience were a true one but she seemed intent upon the fact of herself as if it contained no trace of fiction. So from the day she handed in her story about the dream of the child born with the wooden leg I in the refectory began to watch her instead of watching myself whenever I found myself reciting passages at the table and although she couldn't help but watch me while I was reciting the words that had come to live inside me I couldn't imagine that she watched me because of the words I spoke but for some other reason because a person who lived as true to herself as L— did would know that the words I spoke were a substitute for a part of me that was still missing and so even though she looked at me while I spoke I knew it wasn't the words I spoke that made her look at me but rather the bruise because the bruise was the only part of me that I knew was real and a person like L— could only bear to look at what was real. And even though her intolerance for anything imaginary did not make her a great writer it did make her a real person and there was something so beautiful about how she was able to be a real person that it was difficult for me to stop watching her and so as the words I memorized spoke through me and compelled me to look at L— it became difficult for me to stop wanting to become a real person too.

So once I noticed that L— would look at my bruise while I spoke at the table I could not stop looking at her because I wanted always to see if she really was looking at me and so once I started looking at her often I could sometimes not tell if she was looking at me because she wanted to see the bruise on my forehead or because now that I had begun looking at her every time I spoke at the table she could feel me looking at her first and when she looked at me she could only see the bruise clearly. But even though after a while I couldn't tell if when I began to speak I looked at L— first or if she started to look at my bruise first it still was clear to me that she was always looking at my bruise when she looked at me because I was sure that the bruise was the only real part of me and I was sure that L— would only look at the part of me that was real. And I was so excited that somebody in the world finally noticed a part of me that was real that now when I would begin to speak at the lunch table and look at L— I would also imagine her walking over to me and sweeping the hair out of my eyes and kissing the bruise on my forehead and that made me think that it was really the bruise that made me look at L— because I knew that the bruise came to me because I was lonely and L— was some-one who could help stop me from being lonely. And though there was nothing that I hated more than my friends looking at me during lunch to see how my bruise was doing when I looked at L— I hoped she would look at me and really see the bruise and the way that she looked at me made me hope that she could really see me and see the bruise and the story of my imagination and this would help me finally become a real person.

The DOORKNOB

It wasn't until the night when I was alone in my room and the face in the doorknob started dictating poems to me that I understood what exactly the professor meant when he said something is happening or something isn't happening in a story because that's when I first felt that something I was imagining inside of me changed something in the world outside of me and more than anything when I wrote my first poem I knew that something had to change in the world outside of me though there was nothing that I was scared of more than something changing in the world outside of me. But I knew that as long as I kept writing I could never know the end of what was exactly inside of my imagination and so there was no way I could tell how this would change me or the world outside of me and this scared me but more than anything I wanted to be a writer and so there was nothing I could do except write and be scared.

But before I even saw the face in the doorknob—before I could hear the poem coming inside of me—I watched for several nights the sky outside my window. And though I had sat at my desk in the dormer below the window since the day I moved in I hadn't ever stared at the sky instead of doing my homework. But now suddenly I sat at my desk and I stared at the sky and thought of L— and I didn't do my homework. And there was a part of me that couldn't bear to stare out the window because the sky was so beautiful and I never wanted to see anything beautiful again without L— but I couldn't stop staring out the window because every time I did I thought of her. But after several nights of being so distracted by the sky outside the window that I didn't work but only thought of L— I knew if I were going to graduate I had to move my desk to the front of the room away from the window. But if I hadn't been so distracted I never would have even moved my desk and I never would have seen the face in the doorknob and it is for this reason that I have to believe that the poem that was outside of me wanted to so badly get inside of me that it made the night sky such a shade of blue that I could only think of how beautiful it was each time I saw it and how I would like to look at it with L—. And it is only because of the color of the sky on those nights that I moved my desk from below the window in the dormer where it had stood ever since I first moved into the room to the front wall of the room next to the front door where I could see the brass doorknob out of the left corner of my eye whenever I sat at my desk though before I moved the desk I had no idea that I would be able to see the brass doorknob out of the left corner of my eye.

And it is only because of the distracting color of the sky that I kept the desk there because keeping the desk there against the front wall of the room next to the door blocked the closet door slightly so that the closet door could not open more than thirty-three degrees without hitting the right front edge of the desk. But I kept the desk there because when the desk had been below the window in the dormer I could not stop from turning my head up to look at the sky. And when I saw the color of the sky I thought of L— and how I would like to look at the sky with her. And when I thought of L— I had to turn to face the front door each time someone walked down the hall across the squeaky floorboard outside my door because when I thought about L— I became very nervous that someone wanted to come into my room. And so I would look up from my desk at the night sky and see the intense shade of blue and then think of L— and then hear the squeaky floor-board and then turn around to face the door and on those nights it seemed that it was especially busy in the hall and I was always looking up from my desk at the night sky and then twisting my head around towards the front door because of the squeaky floorboard. It was very difficult to get work done with me having to look up and twist my head around so many times. So I thought if I moved the desk to the front wall of the room at least now I could not look up at the sky but even so I could now not stop myself from looking at the door whenever the floorboard squeaked. And so to tell the truth once I was away from the dormer I had to read in such a way that my head was not completely down so that even though it wasn't completely up my head was up enough to see out of the top corners of my eyes the front door. So even though I was still nervous the fact that I could no longer see the sky and didn't have to think of L— made it easier to manage my fear of the squeaking floorboard if I kept my head a certain way that let me always look at the front door without moving anything except my eyeballs. And I thought this way I would get more work done so even though the desk blocked part of the closet door it didn't matter. I no longer had to look up and turn my head every time the floor squeaked but only look up with my eyes and not my whole head and so the fact that the desk now blocked the closet door slightly seemed irrelevant especially because the closet door still opened wide enough for me to enter the closet normally. And despite the fact that the door was not fully functional I did not have any problems moving from the room into the closet or from the closet into the room and I did not for any reason have to enter the closet sideways. And that's how I knew that the face in the doorknob that made me write the poem had first made me notice the intense blue of the night sky and then hear the floorboard squeak. Because if the sky hadn't been that shade and if the floorboard hadn't squeaked my desk would still be sitting underneath the window in the dormer and I would still not yet understand what it means for something to happen in a story. But I know all that now.

But once I sat down to work at the desk even though I no longer had the problem of twisting my neck to face the door every time I heard the floorboard squeak outside I did meet the face stuck in the doorknob and even though it seemed that I could get more school work done now with only having to move my eyeballs up a little and not my head up and over my shoulder suddenly when I saw her face in the doorknob I couldn't get any work done at all. I could only watch her face because now that it was only her face in the doorknob I didn't feel so scared though I felt a little scared because suddenly

I noticed there was a face in the doorknob but I wasn't too scared. And so I sat at my desk staring at the doorknob instead of doing my school work and it was because her face had such a big mouth that the flesh of the lips just seemed like a thick pink rubber band stretching and although the stretched lips of the mouth were on my doorknob I began to imagine that this mouth in the doorknob wasn't in the doorknob at all but stuck in the side of my face and it was because of the way the lips stretched wide like rubber bands across the doorknob that I thought the mouth was on the side of my face because the lips of the mouth reminded me of a mouth that I had once seen on television—a mouth that was the mouth of a twin who had never separated from the body of her sister but was now only a mouth stuck on the side of the sister's face.

And the mouth that was stuck on the side of the sister's face on television flashed its teeth from the hole it made in its sister's cheek so that when I saw the mouth stuck in the sister's face I thought of a rabid dog that had come to bite the flesh from the sister's face but instead had fallen into the face and was trapped in the same face it had wanted to eat and so now it could do nothing but bark and flash teeth but of course this wasn't the story of the mouth on the side of the sister's face because the mouth had never been a dog but only a twin that had never become a real twin but just a mouth on the side of a head that already had a mouth and so when I looked at the face in the brass doorknob I could only think it was my twin sister that had come to spook my head with her mouth.

But the child stuck with the barking hole in the side of her face wasn't at all spooked by the mouth and she called the mouth *Sister* and when the mouth spoke in its strange tongue the girl fingered its lips to calm it and she translated its words so that her parents could understand what her sister needed. For example she would say *My sister would like a glass of milk* and then a hand from off camera would put a glass of milk to the second mouth. And instead of swallowing the milk the mouth would suck and spit and the milk would streak down the girl's face and the girl wouldn't say anything but only sit there with her hands folded in her lap letting her sister drink her milk as she pleased. And then the mouth—when it was done drinking the milk—the mouth opened and closed and opened and closed and the little girl said *My sister is tired* and stuck her finger in the mouth. And the mouth grunted and sighed and slowly started to suck the digit that the sister had given her to suck. And so when I first saw the face in the doorknob even though I was scared of the face in the doorknob I thought that maybe I should give her my finger to suck. And then I thought that if I just pretended the face in the doorknob wasn't there I could do my homework and so when I sat at my desk and the floorboard squeaked though I very much wanted to look up and make sure no one was bursting into my room I didn't look up. I didn't let my eyeballs move. I kept my neck locked and nothing in me turned. I would not let my neck turn. I knew that if my neck turned I would see the reflection of my sister's face in the doorknob. I knew I would start rubbing the hole in the side of my face to calm her down. And more than the floorboard squeaking my sister spook would stop me from working. Sticking my fingers in the hole in the side of my face would never let me forget who I was and more than anything I didn't want a spook in the side of my face to force me to be who I was. I thought that if I could not let myself forget who I was while I sat at my desk it would be impossible to keep reading or writing anything.

But then once I thought to check to see if the face in the doorknob was still there because I began to hope that she was just a story in my imagination and she would when I looked up finally no longer be there but when I looked up and stared into the brass doorknob she was of course there and her lips were moving. And though each time I had looked up at her I could see her lips moving I until this time had never heard her say anything even though her lips were always moving and this time when I looked up and saw the face in the doorknob I heard things in my head. I heard words and even though I heard the words I knew I was only hearing them in my head so I thought I should write them down because like anything that was just in my head these words could disappear. And I thought if my sister was trying to tell me something I should make sure her words wouldn't disappear and they didn't. When I wrote them down they looked like this:

I want to stop
keeping my body
settled
like a teacup
in a dust store.

And if the words on the page—if the words on the page hadn't broken into lines like a poem I would have thought the words were just a message. But even though the lines of the words broke like a poem I still thought it was a message because there was a wanting in the lines and I couldn't ignore that my sister spook was wanting something from me even though there was something in the words that made them pretty like a poem and therefore easy to ignore because no one listens to poetry. Who thinks a poem is a hand-delivered message? Only the crazy poets who drink themselves to death and I didn't think I was crazy and I never liked the taste of alcohol. But I did always like the sound of words and how the sound of words could make you almost say anything if you followed the sound long enough like *Fee Fie Foe Fum stick your thumb into the sun* even though I had never thought about my thumb and the sun before but only knew how to run through the sounds *Fee Fie Foe Fum etc.* But even so I was a student of literature and knew how to make poems mean what they meant as words and nothing more than words and keep everything under control by reducing a poem into a contradictory meaning due to syntax or ambiguous grammar and therefore null and void and then moving on to another poem in the anthology. But when I wrote down these words that the doorknob had given me because I knew I had written them because I could see the words come out of me onto the page and I could see my own hand put the words onto the page I knew that I was my own sister. I knew that these words were my own words and when I saw what I wanted I couldn't doubt any longer that something was happening to me. I could no longer believe that my thoughts were just thoughts and could slip away into a dream and be forgotten because now there was this thing here and it was mine and I had written it. And I could only think now that things might for once really change because what was happening on the inside of me was suddenly sitting on my desk outside of me and that's how I learned how to make something happen in a story. And when I finished writing my poem and thinking about how writing the poem was finally making something happen in my life I could only go to the cafeteria and steal a glass of milk and place it in front of the brass doorknob so I could stop getting messages from my sister spook for a little while because this message was already too much for me. I knew that I couldn't handle any more things happening in my life than this one little poem would make happen and so I wanted to give her a glass of milk to keep her busy while I dealt with things starting to happen to me. And that's how I started to learn how to write a story.

The SENTENCE

Two years earlier I had found a sentence in an essay and ever since I had found the sentence I had kept it written neatly by hand on the lined side of an index card that I had cut to the exact size of a business card so that I could keep the sentence in my wallet in the plastic protective plastic that was meant to protect credit cards bank cards drivers licenses student ids family photos and especially certain business cards of great importance but that I had used primarily to protect this particular sentence that I had found in an essay two years earlier while reading the essay for my literature class. I can't remember what the essay was called or who had written it or why we had even read the essay—what its relationship was to the novels we were reading. I can remember even less of what the essay was about because when I read the essay I was a very young student of literature and there was very little that I understood about literature at all and whenever I was asked to read an essay about literature I rarely understood anything in the essay but I was stubborn and would always read the essay to the end because I thought if I forced myself to read the things students of literature were supposed to read even if I didn't understand the things as I was reading eventually I would understand them and I would be a student of literature and that is how I read this essay and so I had understood next to nothing that was written in this essay and I had understood very little of what my professor had to say about the essay too but somehow I thought to write this one sentence from the essay down and to keep it with me always.

And I thought as long as I kept looking at the sentence one day I would eventually know what it meant to me—why I had written down this sentence and put it on a card that I kept with me always in my wallet and so when I was waiting in line at the refectory or standing on the corner by the library waiting for the night shuttle or sitting on the steps outside the Blue Room in between classes I would pull out my wallet and read the card to myself and see if I had yet really understood the sentence and slowly I began to realize the reason that this sentence had been important to me was because it had nothing to do with literature but with real life and what it discussed was something in life I didn't yet myself know and so each time I read *Each time a man speaks to another in an authentic and full manner...something takes place which changes the nature of the two beings present* it was as if I were reading a sentence that was discussing something imaginary that was happening between two people in a story but of course I knew the speaking that the sentence was talking about was not the speaking of two people in a story but the speaking between two people in real life and I wondered if I could ever speak to someone in such a way and the more I wondered about such things the lonelier I felt as if I had never spoken to anyone ever before. And so each time I pulled out the card to stare at my sentence I wondered when I would ever begin to speak in such a way and the more I thought that I wanted to speak to someone in a very real way the more scared I got that I never would be able to because I thought there were so many real things to say to someone that it seemed impossible to say them all and without saying them all it seemed as if somehow what one said was untrue because without finding sentences for all the thoughts in my head there would only be some parts of thoughts and that would not be true because it seemed each of the thoughts helped make a whole world and it seemed if I didn't find enough sentences for all the thoughts in my head I would never really be able to live in the same world with somebody and more than anything I wanted to live in the same world with somebody and so soon I stopped looking at the sentence altogether because it made me think it would be impossible ever to have enough sentences to speak to somebody in a real way and I might be stuck alone in my thoughts for a very long time.

The SOUTH ENTRANCE

One thing I began to learn that year was that although I could choose if or when I would change the way I did something at school I could not choose if or when another person changed the way she did something at school. And if and when she did change the way she did something at school even though I myself hadn't chosen to change a single thing I had been doing the way that I did that thing at school would now have to change too.

To be sure there was almost nothing that I did at school that I chose to change and I especially never thought to change nor chose to change the way that I ate lunch at school and the way that I ate lunch at school on Monday through Friday was the same way each of those days beginning with Monday and ending with Friday and then on Saturday and Sunday there was a different way that I ate but on both Saturday and Sunday I ate on both days differently the same way but differently than on Monday through Friday but that's another story. And when I say that I ate lunch the same way on Monday and Friday and all the days in between that's not to say that I ate the same thing every day and what I mean about the way I ate lunch has not so much to do with eating as it does with the things that needed to happen before eating. And even though I had a certain set of classes on Monday Wednesday and Friday that were different from the set of classes that I had on Tuesday and Thursday I was lucky enough to have class on each of those days ending at 11:50 a.m. even though the classes on Monday Wednesday and Friday started at 11:00 a.m. and the classes on Tuesday and Thursday started at 10:30 a.m. So I was able to enter the refectory on Monday Wednesday and Friday and also on Tuesday and Thursday at exactly noon and I knew that it was always at exactly noon because when I entered the first set of doors of the refectory I could hear the campus bell tolling. And although I had two sets of entrances to choose from—the north entrance and the south entrance—in order to enter the refectory I always chose to enter through the south entrance doors because they were furthest from the main walkway and although I had to walk about fifty paces further to reach these doors few students coming off the main walkway would want to walk the extra fifty paces and therefore there was never a long line to get into the refectory at this door and I could be sure that I would enter the first set of doors just as the noon bells were tolling. And I would always enter through the northernmost of the four south entrance doors not only because it was the closest south entrance door to the walkway but because the refectory worker who checked our meal cards sat at a table at the next set of doors which separated the south entrance foyer from the refectory proper and the cafeteria worker's table was always set at the northernmost door of this next set of doors that separated the south entrance foyer from the refectory proper so if I entered the northernmost of the four south entrance doors once I entered through it the door would immediately place me in the short line that formed in the south entrance foyer and I would not be cut off in line by anyone entering any of the other more southern doors of the south entrance who would then have to cross the length of the foyer in order to reach the line.

And because a majority of the students at school including me were in the habit of going to lunch right after classes ended at 11:50 it was my impression that I wasn't the only student who always entered the refectory through the same door at the same time no matter what day of the school week it was because it seemed that as I made my way to the northernmost door of the south entrance and once I entered into the south entrance foyer and waited to be admitted to lunch through the northernmost of the south entrance doors that separated the south entrance foyer from the refectory proper and was manned by a single refectory worker I was almost positive that the same faces were both behind me and in front of me in line each time in exactly the same places. And it was because each of us did our part to arrive in line at the same time and same place every day that I was allowed to have lunch the same way every day Monday through Friday and I was grateful to these other students who were also very careful to eat lunch the same way every day Monday through Friday.

But it wasn't until one day when someone who did not normally stand behind me in the lunch line at the south entrance to the refectory stood behind me in the lunch line at the south entrance to the refectory that I realized that it didn't matter if I was careful to eat lunch the same way every day because if someone else decided to eat lunch a different way and stand behind me in line in the south entrance foyer of the refectory she was not only changing the way that she ate lunch but she was also changing the way that I ate lunch. But I didn't understand this fact until I heard behind me in the lunch line at the south entrance foyer of the refectory an unfamiliar voice say *Hello M—* and when I turned around and saw L— there standing at noon in the lunch line in the south entrance foyer of the refectory where I had never seen her stand before even though I stood there every day Monday through Friday I could do nothing except helplessly say *Hello* back. And even though after a few seconds of awkward silence she asked me about the bruise on my forehead even though I was happy that she finally asked me about the bruise on my forehead there was a part of me that was scared to find her standing there because even though I had wanted her always to ask me about the bruise on my forehead I knew now I would never eat lunch the same way again no matter how carefully I was to enter the northernmost door of the south entrance of the refectory exactly at noon.

The WOOL COAT

I had found the wool coat in the closet of my dormitory on the day that I moved in and although it was not my coat I immediately felt drawn to it and soon thought of it as my coat and then I wore it all the time. The fabric of the wool coat— an orange and black plaid— made me think that the wool coat was in fact a hunter's coat. But the shade of the orange in the plaid of the wool coat was a very natural shade of orange an orange not very different from the orange that I had seen in the autumn leaves and because of the naturalness of this particular shade of orange wool—which was rather bright but not unnaturally bright—not brighter than any possible shade of natural orange—I could have never worn the wool coat for a walk in the woods during hunting season. For this reason it was obvious that the wool coat was not a hunter's coat though because of the orange and black plaid I could not help but think of it as a hunter's coat. Each time I saw the orange in the pattern of the plaid wool from which the coat was made the color had the strange effect of making me think both that the coat was a hunter's coat and that it was not a hunter's coat and could never be a hunter's coat.

The wool coat which both did and did not look like a hunter's coat was regardless of the effect of the orange plaid by all means a man's coat but because of my girlish face whenever I wore the coat I did not look like a man but rather I looked like a boy with a girlish face. The body of the coat was a straight rectangle and because the coat was a little large for me (it was sized for a man) the fabric of the coat fell straight down the sides of my body just past my hips erasing both the curves of my hips and the curves of my breasts and though I often wore men's clothes that made me look boyish I had never been mistaken for a boy. I simply looked like a girl in boys' clothes. But when at that moment I looked at myself in the mirror while wearing the wool coat I thought that if I wore the wool coat now for my walk with L— someone might call me sir and then certainly L— would know that I was attracted to her and realize that our walk was a date because I had wanted to think of it as a date. But even though I had been called sir only once before while wearing the wool coat I don't believe that the person who called me sir had mistaken me for a man but rather for a boy because despite the fact that the coat had erased the curves of my hips and breasts it obviously had not erased the girlishness of my face and only a boy could have such a girlish face. And because L— knew me I was sure that L— would not mistake me for a boy but I realized that in wearing the wool coat on our walk I took the chance that she could mistake me for a girl who looked like a boy who looked like a girl. She could mistake me for a girl who would think of a walk with another girl as something more than a walk and though this made me nervous it did not make me choose another coat to wear.

The TREES

It was already a long time dark on campus when I got to the statue of Marcus Aurelius at the top of the lower green though it wasn't very late. It had been dark already for three hours since before dinner and the bell had just rung eight times on the top of Sayles Hall and I could hear the voices of the students who ate later or took longer to eat than I did coming out of the refectory though the refectory was behind the buildings that flanked the right side of the green. The voices echoed off the brick so far that I could hear them at the top of the lower green and I could hear the steady creaking and slamming of the refectory door.

Standing there alone I started to like the sound: the creak and then the slam and then the new voices rising into the air.

The whole of the operation sounded like a strange old machine—a contraption that existed to sound off just at that hour and place so I couldn't forget where I was standing and who I was and so I just stood there and listened and for a few minutes I forgot why I was standing there and I didn't feel nervous.

Then the voices came towards me and soon a few of them passed me on the walkway though I was standing in the grass and the grass left wet marks on my leather shoes and the voices moved up the hill past the main green towards the Rockefeller Library and when they passed me I put my hands in the pockets of my wool coat and hung my head down but still every now and then someone who knew me would pass and say *Hey, M—, aren't you going to the Rock?* And I would answer *No, not tonight.* But I felt embarrassed saying that so I added *Maybe later.* And then Emily walked by with her books in hand and stopped and walked over to me and said *What are you doing here?* And I said *I'm going on a walk.* And she didn't say anything else. She just looked me hard in the eyes and turned around and continued walking towards the library and when she looked at me I knew that she knew everything.

When everyone passed I walked out of the grass to the walkway. There weren't any leaves left on the trees and they rose up black against the sky—so black they made me see the sky was blue even at night. And behind the trees I could see the top floor of the library all lit up. I could see the chairs in the windows and slowly I could see the bodies fill the chairs in the windows. And the sound of the creaking and slamming of the refectory door had stopped and there was only the sound of the wind and the lights of the library in the distance and I was standing there alone now and still L— hadn't come to meet me at the statue of Marcus Aurelius. I started to feel cold and was glad that I had worn my wool cap too.

And there was something about standing there alone after all the sounds had passed after everyone had moved on to the library and left me there on the lower green on the pavement in the cold that made me need to talk to L— even though she wasn't there even though there was no sign of her being there and even though I couldn't imagine ever really talking to her I started to imagine talking to her in an imaginary way as if she were a story I invented for myself as I stood there in the cold waiting for something I couldn't imagine and so I began walking in circles around the statue of Marcus Aurelius watching the grass slap wet against my shoes. And since part of me felt that L— could in some real way hear me I was nervous before I began to speak but I didn't want my nervousness to affect the things I had wanted to say to her so I tried to push myself away from the words and let the words fall as they needed to from my tongue. It was difficult to start because it wasn't as if the words were waiting but there was only a feeling in my gut and it needed to come out of me and I knew the feeling needed words to come out but at first the only word of real feeling I could extract from myself was her name and so for several seconds I stood there repeating her name: *L— L— L—*. Until finally the feeling freed itself inside the words and I said *L— have you ever seen the rain run down the slate roofs of the dorms—the rain rolling down the black-gray stone of the building across the way while looking out the window of your room late at night? How the gutters sometimes are stuffed with leaves in the fall and because of the tree near the door the water comes down heavier exactly above the entrance. Have you ever felt glad that you were the person already inside and not the poor soul coming in late from the grad student bar or the library fumbling for your key half drunk with beer or words stuck in the steady drip that wets your back the drip that will follow you cold into bed? Weren't you glad that you came back from the library early and sat at your own desk safely working? But I'm sure you know there's nothing safe about working. The poems can get to you. The words the way they become the things themselves if the rhythm is right. The page disappears. The page disappears and then the angel—she's holding on to you—and you can feel the fear as if it were real and breathing on you. Imagine her size, L—. Imagine a creature so large needing to hold onto you. It makes me dizzy just thinking about it. Do you like pastries, L—? Maybe we can go to a cafe one day and eat pastries. Warm pastries topped with cream. Something we would never find in the refectory. Someplace where no one from the refectory would ever go. A place just for you and me and strangers in elegant overcoats sipping coffee. Wouldn't that be nice? I bet you think that would be nice. I think it's nice, L—. Do you think it could be like that? Just nice? Not scary. L—. L—. L—.*

But when I said her name no one answered. I was only speaking the sentences to myself and they sounded artificial as if they weren't the real sentences for the feeling. I was worried that they were just thoughts I made for the voice and I wondered what my real thoughts were and I worried that I made the wrong words come out of my mouth. I worried that I wanted them to sound as if they were coming out of a book—a real book that was my own. A book I had written. A book that was so beautiful someone would want to read it. Someone could fall into it and get lost because the words were so beautiful someone would want to listen to them. She would want to listen to the words. L— would want to listen. But she wasn't even there and I was worried that even so the words just sounded stupid.

It was twenty-five after eight and I thought about leaving and started to think about my seat in the library. I wondered if anyone was sitting in it because if ever I were studying in the library I was always careful to be in my seat by 7:30 because there was only one seat where I could study in the library and if I were to go there after eight there was a good chance that my seat would be occupied and then there would be no place for me to study in the library and I would have to walk back across campus to my room and sit in my hard wooden chair and study alone.

My library seat was a vinyl-covered reclining seat—a seat in the periodicals room the entrance to which was on the right-hand side off the lobby across from the circulation desk. The seat wasn't visible when one first entered the periodicals room and to get to the seat one had to walk straight ahead past all the reading tables through the stacks to the back wall of the periodicals room. But the back wall of the periodicals room wasn't a wall at all but a giant window that at night when it was dark outside and light inside acted as a mirror. My reclining chair was the third reclining chair from the left wall of the room—a cinderblock wall—and my chair faced the windows. And the reason I chose this chair as my library chair was that when I sat in the chair I could watch myself in the window as I read and I liked the way I looked when I read in this chair because when I saw myself read I knew I looked like a student not only because I sat in the chair with a book in my hand but because behind me you could see the stacks filled with literary journals and behind the stacks you could see the other students leaning over the reading tables and working and even though I couldn't see List Art Center I knew if I had ever been in my chair during the day I would have a perfect view of List Art Center which was right across the street from this side of the library. Somehow it seemed important that as a student of literature I read my books in view of the art center and if the picture of myself that I saw in the window at night was an actual photograph anyone who could have seen the photograph would not have doubted that I was a student of literature because there I was clearly in a library reading my poetry and my prose and what pleased me most about this seat in the library was that I had always wanted to be a student of literature and then there I was in the window no doubt a student of literature.

But now standing in the grass at the foot of the statue of Marcus Aurelius I was scared because I didn't know how to return to the library knowing that my seat was most likely no longer still empty for me. And when I imagined myself walking into the periodicals room only to find another person there reading and staring at herself in the window I felt a hollowness inside myself as if everything that was real inside me had disappeared and there was nothing but a shell of me with my face slapped onto it holding nothing. And when I looked up and saw the trees and the buildings silent around me I was out of place as if suddenly school was a dream and I had just become aware of wandering through it. I wondered if there was somewhere in the world another world to which I could belong and how would I ever get there without losing my seat in the library.

If only L— hadn't looked at the bruise on my forehead or if only she hadn't made me think she could really see me or if she wasn't now almost thirty minutes late I would still maybe be myself. But now I had to wonder if she had ever looked at me at all or if she had just focused on the bruise in the way that a thinking person focuses on a bright light on a wall—the kind of focus that has nothing to do with seeing but only to do with relaxing your eyes so you can fall deeper into yourself. And I was worried now that she was not interested in seeing me and not interested in making a place for me in the world but that in agreeing to see her I had risked the only place I had in the world. And even though at that moment I knew L— maybe was not interested in trying to see me in a real way I more than anything needed her to arrive even if she had no intention of ever looking at my bruise or listening to a single sentence I spoke because if she didn't arrive I would be forced to attempt to resume my usual evening study habits. And now that it was so late I dreaded the prospect of going to the library without any books and finding a stranger sitting in my chair in the periodicals room because then I would be forced to accept the fact that school had gone on without me. And in just a few minutes the chair that taught me that I was a student of literature would simply abandon me for another student body and more than anything I was scared to learn that it wasn't important that I in particular had sat in this seat and studied literature but that it was for the school simply important that someone sat in this seat and studied. And more than anything I had to be careful to avoid situations that let me see that school would always continue being with or without me because I could not imagine where or what I would be if I were not at school. And I was very scared to realize that in the end it didn't matter to the school if I were a student here or not and if that didn't matter to the school it was important for L— to show up soon especially because I could not bear to realize that I was unimportant both to L— and to school on the same night because then I would not know where my place in the world was anymore at all.

I was circling the statue of Marcus Aurelius wondering if tomorrow I would be able to return to the library and if

I would be different tomorrow when I arrived at my seat in the library—different because I had left the library and my studies to see if it was possible to talk to another person in a real way—in a way that was as real as the imaginary talking in books—and since it seemed that it would not be possible for me to talk to L— in a real way tonight I circled the statue of Marcus Aurelius and wondered if the words in my books tomorrow would seem more or less real and because I was circling the back of the statue of Marcus Aurelius wondering about all this just as L— arrived at 8:30 I didn't notice at first that it was actually L— coming out of a small path in between the two buildings that lined the left side of the lower green.

There was no one else around as she came out of the small path in between two buildings wearing a long black overcoat. A wool overcoat made for a girl. The kind of overcoat you might see someone's grandmother wearing in a photograph as she waited for someone's grandfather to come back from the war. An overcoat tapered at the waist. But the overcoat was just a little too short to be her overcoat. It was too short to be her overcoat so the skirt that she wore under it hung out from below the overcoat and flitted against her legs which were covered in thick blue tights and because the coat was too short I knew it really wasn't her overcoat. Her wrists stuck out of the sleeves. There was no one coming home from a war. And her head was down. But her hair was up. Not straight up but pressed up on the side. Lopsided. The way someone's hair is matted and forced up while being pressed against a pillow during sleep. It was up as if she had just woken up. But it wasn't straight up. It was too long to stick straight up. And when she finally did look up the lights above the pathway flashed her eyes and they shone black. They might have scared me if her face wasn't swollen with sleep. Wasn't so childlike. If she didn't blink so long and often. Or if her skin wasn't still creased from sheets. She came up close to me. And I could see the faintest freckles on her skin and because her skin was so white and her eyes so dark and the brown of her hair was a bit reddish and her coat was too small I thought for a moment that she was a Russian schoolgirl. And if she was a Russian schoolgirl why couldn't I now in my wool coat be a Russian school boy? That's what I was thinking. And I was surprised when she opened her mouth and spoke English to me. But I wasn't that surprised. I hadn't imagined us Russian for very long.

And when she spoke she was sheepish and she looked at the ground when she said *Sorry I'm late. I fell asleep and missed dinner and only woke up at 8:15.* And then she bit her lower lip and looked up at me and smiled a crooked smile which wasn't much of a smile but more like a place holder as if to say if I were to smile it would be here but it wasn't a real smile and then she looked down again and put her hand in her coat pocket and kept it there for a few seconds and then she looked up at me again and pulled a strange looking apple from her pocket and said *I brought this for you. We should eat it now.* And I didn't say anything but only watched her take the apple in both hands and when I looked at her hands I noticed that they were small and delicate almost like a child's with slender fingers that seemed hardly strong enough to break open the apple but she did break it open with her bare hands and when she did I realized it wasn't an apple at all but something more magical because the inside of the apple sparkled with small ruby flesh like tiny red tooth-shaped crystals hanging off a dull stone wall and they sparkled under the lights and when I saw the sparkle of the apple I realized it wasn't an apple at all but a pomegranate.

And L— took one half of the fruit to her mouth and sucked at the red parts and with her other hand she handed me the other half of the fruit and when her lips pulled off the fruit her mouth was red and dirty. But I didn't know what to do with my half of the fruit because it seemed strange to suck on the pomegranate there on the lower green at the foot of the statue of Marcus Aurelius with the wind whipping and everyone else studying in the library so I picked a few of the red seeds out with my fingers and put them in my mouth and the seeds were more sour than sweet and I could feel my throat close a little from the sourness but there was something about the taste of the seeds that made me think that if I kept eating I might find a very sweet seed even though they were very sour but I didn't find a sweet one and then all my seeds were gone and my fingers were dirty so I threw the shell of the pomegranate in the grass and wiped my fingers on the inside of my pockets and wiped my mouth on the sleeve of my coat and watched L—. She had finished eating all the red seeds inside the fruit too but instead of throwing the shell of the fruit away she ran the tip of her tongue over the white cavities where the small ruby seeds had been and licked up the juice they had left behind and for some reason the sight of that made me look away. And when I looked back at her she was looking at me and she smiled a crooked smile but I only looked away and didn't know what to say but luckily she said we should start walking because it was too cold to stand in place and so we started walking and once we started walking I didn't feel so strange because we were walking around campus and I didn't have to watch L— run her tongue over anything and I loved walking around campus because its paths were organized in such a way that even though one often felt as though a path were leading one astray into the unknown each path no matter how mysterious in its appearance always in some way led one back to the statue of Marcus Aurelius. And that's also why I loved the statue of Marcus Aurelius.

We wandered along the paths until one led us to the main green and we didn't say very much to each other as we walked but we said some things but mostly they were the things people said when they didn't know how to say something real to each other but then L— surprised me and when we got to the main green she started walking off the path to the center of the main green towards the strange sculpture that was there and I followed her even though I had always disliked the sculpture and what I had always disliked about this sculpture was that it didn't make any sense. I didn't understand its shape so I didn't understand its meaning. Its reason for being there wasn't clear the way Marcus Aurelius's reason for being was clear and that was the reason I didn't find it beautiful and I'm not sure that anyone else found it actually beautiful but I think that they only found it comfortable because it sat on the center of the main green and it was basin-shaped almost like a cradle made of iron and on any given day with a bit of sunshine there was always someone sitting in it reading but now it was dark and cold and when we arrived at the statue L— suggested that we sit in it and I couldn't understand why she wanted to sit in this statue—in this cold iron cradle—but I didn't want to tell L— that I didn't like the statue because I was too nervous to explain why I didn't like the statue and so I agreed with her and went to sit in the statue and I wondered if sitting with her in the statue meant that I would be forced to kiss her in the statue because I couldn't understand why anyone would sit in a cold iron statue at night with someone else without a definite purpose so

I became scared of any purposes L— might have and I began to think of what they might be and the only purpose I could think of was kissing and this made me uncomfortable. But since I didn't want L— to know that I thought of our walk as a date I pretended that I was not scared of her and not scared of kissing her and I went with her to sit in the cold iron cradle of a statue.

But when I got to the foot of the statue I couldn't make myself sit in the cradle of the statue because I was afraid that if I sat in the cradle of the statue L— would sit there next to me and the cradle was small enough that if two people sat in it their bodies would most definitely be touching. So I sat on the base that the cradle stood on and just as I had guessed L— jumped into the cradle of the statue and stared at the stars and the ends of her overcoat and skirt flitted in the wind off the edge of the statue and she flopped her head back and stared at the stars and since she stared at the stars I stared at the trees which led into the stars and what I liked about staring at the trees on campus at night was that now with no leaves they looked black and even though it was already dark their blackness against the sky showed me that the sky was truly blue and not black even at night and the trees on campus showed me this each year from late fall to the end of winter but I was still always surprised when I saw it and then I was glad to know from the trees that the sky was always blue and that's why I thought the trees at night were so beautiful.

And just as I was enjoying the blackness of the trees against the blueness of the sky L— asked me a question. She said *Aren't the stars beautiful* but since I hadn't been looking at the stars I hadn't thought to think they were beautiful. I only knew that the trees were beautiful because they were here to show me that the sky was always blue and I wondered why she thought to ask me if the stars were beautiful when it appeared as though she had been sitting in the cradle staring at the stars although maybe she too was staring at the trees and watching how they ended in the sky. But I didn't tell her that I thought all that. I only said *I don't know but I like the trees. I like the trees because they're black. I like how black they are because they're black enough to show me that the sky is always blue even at night. I like that. I like knowing that* and I don't know what made me say this because it was one of the many kinds of things that I thought but never told anyone and it made me nervous that I had said something I had thought but before I could finish feeling nervous L— said *I think that every time I look at the trees too once they've lost their leaves and the winter is coming* and I was suddenly shocked that she had said that because it sounded a little like one of my thoughts and suddenly I looked at her mouth and wondered how it could say something that I thought too and when I looked at her mouth I saw that it was still stained from the pomegranate and even though her mouth was stained her lips looked small and sweet. But when I realized that I thought her lips looked small and sweet I felt a little ill and because I felt a little ill I also felt the need to try to ask her a question so she wouldn't think anything was wrong with me but it was hard for me to think of a question I wanted to ask her because it was hard to feel ill and think at the same time so I couldn't think of a question so I just asked her any question. I asked her if she liked poetry and she said yes. And then I felt a little more ill and suddenly I also felt the need to ask another question but again it was hard to think and feel at the same time so I just asked her if she liked angels and she asked me if I meant in poetry or in life and I said both and she didn't laugh. She thought it was a serious question. And it made me more ill when she didn't laugh at my strange question. And when she answered she answered seriously. She said yes and then she asked me if I liked angels in poetry and in real life and she didn't laugh when she asked me and the more she didn't laugh the sicker I felt. But I didn't tell her that I felt sick. I only said I didn't know if I liked them. I only knew that I was interested in them but I could not yet say whether I liked them. And then I didn't feel like looking at L—'s lips anymore or the trees. I only liked looking down at the grass but when I looked down at the grass I thought about my bruise and when I thought about my bruise I felt it ache. I felt it ache and it made me feel lonely and suddenly when I felt myself feel lonely I could only think that someone else was sitting in my chair at the library now and there was no other place for me to go.

A DRUGSTORE COMB

In literature class I had learned that memories didn't live in people but in things. I learned that the only way for a person to recover her memories was for her to see the right things. I learned that if a person did not see the right things in the world (things that made her remember her memories) it was as if she had never been born because she would have no memory of having been born and a person with no memory of having been born was someone who could have no memory of having lived and therefore was not someone who had lived but someone who was simply living and so if a person did not see the right things in the world it was as if she had never been born. And I was told for this reason that something as simple as a plastic drugstore comb had the power to give or not give a person her life back. But since only memories could prove to someone that she had existed before the present moment (since only memories in this way could prove that she had ever been born) a person with no memories could also never die because in order to die a person had to be born first. So I had learned that although something as simple as a plastic drugstore comb could decide whether or not a person could be born a simple plastic drugstore comb could not make a person die unless it let her be born first. So if a thing decided never to give a person her memories back it was as if the thing had also let her live forever because although she could not live without memory—if she could not live it stood to reason that she also could not die.

And when I learned this I knew right away that I had come to school to never die because although school was filled with so many different things there had never been anything at school that had ever reminded me of anything that I had known before I came to school and because this was true I could only believe that I was sent to school so that I would never die.

And I knew I would never die each time I looked at the trees at night because when I looked at the trees at night it was as if I were looking at the trees for the very first time because each time I looked at the trees at night what I saw so resembled what I had seen every other time that I had looked at the trees at night that it was as if each time I had looked at the trees it was the same time and so it felt as if there had only been one time I had ever looked at the trees—no past or present but only always this one moment of looking at the trees at night at school—and whenever I did look at the trees at night at school not only did I see the same thing but I also thought the same thing. I thought that the trees were so black that they showed me the sky was blue even at night and even this thought helped me believe that nothing changed at school because it was always the same thought and even what I thought proved to me that nothing changed because my thoughts showed me that the sky even when it seemed to darken was still blue and would always be blue no matter what color I thought it was and the trees were there not to remind me of a time when the sky had been a different color but to remind me that even now with the sun down nothing was different: the sky was blue. So I knew the trees existed to show me that no matter what day it was it would always be the same day or almost the same day and for this reason since I arrived at school I felt as though I would never die. I would just continue looking at the trees forever.

But now when I looked at the trees on campus they were no longer trees but memories of trees and the blackness of the trees on campus no longer reminded me that the sky was always blue even at night but rather it reminded me of sitting with L— and looking at the trees that first night and how up until that night whenever I looked at the trees I had felt that I had been seeing everything that there was to see but now that I had looked at the trees with L— I wasn't so sure because only that night when I had been with L— did I really see that the stars were above the tips of the trees and only then did I think of how the sky and stars reached behind my head where I could no longer see and of how the sky and stars fell back into the ground behind where the grass had started in the dirt and it was in this way that L— pointed out to me that there had been so much that I hadn't seen or hadn't wanted to see and this made me nervous because suddenly for the first time the trees at night stopped showing me what was and began showing me what wasn't.

So now when I looked at the trees at night they only reminded me that I was alone and that things could change at school because now when I looked at the trees I thought of the time I looked at them with L— but now when I looked at the trees because L— was in her house and not looking at them with me the trees showed me that a person could be with someone and then be alone and although this memory of L— and me and the trees was not a memory of a time before school but only a memory of a particular time at school the fact that I suddenly had memories at school at all and the fact that I knew from literature class that a person with memories was a person who had been born I knew suddenly for the first time that I had been born and that because I had been born now I would also die.

And soon I began to doubt that anything was itself—was anything except memories—because I saw for the first time that the trees were not themselves but only memories of themselves and so I was scared that other things would stop being themselves and turn into memories too and very soon other things did stop being themselves and these other things when they stopped being themselves turned into memories too. But the memories I had were memories of things that I had seen before and so even my memories made me doubt at first that I had any real memories because I wondered if imagining a thing that I had seen before without feeling any feelings while imagining the thing was even a memory at all or only a picture list of things I had seen before. But at night all these memories that at first did not seem to be memories at all—all these things would come alive in my head as I looked at the ceiling in the dark of my dorm room and I could not sleep because the memories I had of these things only led to memories of other things and at first it seemed that these memories of things were coming not to make me feel anything but only to let me know that I had seen things. But the more I thought of these things the less I could see these things and only feel things I had felt before but forgotten.

And so at night in the dark of my room I could see the cans in the weeds. Cans in the weeds along the highway and once I saw the highway I could see the car and I could see my thighs sweaty sticking to the plastic seat of the car. I could see the dark red plastic of the seat and when I looked up I could see the plastic of the radio face. And once I could see the plastic of the radio face I could hear. I could hear that no one was talking or one person was talking. And the one person that was talking said *Let's stop here.* And when I heard the person say *Let's stop here* I could look up from the sentence I was reading and when I saw that I was reading I could see the words that I had been reading. I could see *When they reached the Achilles Statue she turned round. There was pity in her eyes that became laughter on her lips* and I could turn my head up from the book and towards the steering wheel and I could see my father with his hands on the wheel and when I turned my head back down again I could read *'I am sixteen,' he answered, 'and I know what I am about.'* And on the radio I could hear *Hey do you want to take our caller and see what he's got to say? O surely. Go ahead Chuck. Hello Chuck. Yes hello Chuck. Ok this is Tom from Clearwater. When Joey Brown was in Las Vegas he said a dime here a dime there first thing you know you've got twenty cents. That's right. How did you figure that out Tom. Tom must stay up late to figure out stuff like that. I'll tell you that.* And when I remembered hearing *I'll tell you that* I remembered *Let's stop here* and I remembered the gas station and when I remembered the gas station I saw the egg salad sandwich. The egg salad sandwich that came in a white plastic sleeve. The triangular white plastic sleeve that held the egg salad sandwich. The egg salad sandwich that was diagonally cut in half and the sticker on the sleeve of the egg salad sandwich that said *Egg salad sandwich bread: enriched flour water yeast high fructose corn syrup salt vegetable shortening sugar dextrose wheat gluten soy flour calcium propionate corn starch ascorbic acid L-cysteine potassium iodate azodicathbonaride enzyme vegetable and monodiglycerides yeast nutrient (ammonium sulfate). Egg salad: egg celery mayonnaise (soybean oil egg yolks water high fructose corn syrup distilled vinegar) salt spices disodium EDTA celery cracker meal (bleached wheat flour) MSG spice sodium benzoatem potassium sorbate.* And then for a moment I couldn't see anything and I thought that I would fall asleep and when I felt myself falling asleep I saw the knit blanket on top of me and when I saw the blanket I turned and looked up and saw the beige velveteen of the couch and I could hear the sound of the silverware clanking in the other room and when I heard the clanking of silverware I turned and looked up straight ahead of me and I saw Muskovites. I saw Muskovites inside the static of the television like buffalos in big hats and then I didn't see anything.

And then I saw the wheelbarrow. The rusty red wheelbarrow. And I saw that I had filled the wheelbarrow with water. And once I saw the water I could see the dead bird. I could see the dead bird in my hands. I saw one hand lifting a dead wing in the water and the other hand holding the dead body. And I saw the small shovel and the dirt and I saw myself putting the dead washed bird in the dirt. And the bird was the first thing that I saw in my memories to give me a feeling and the feeling was a hollow feeling and the feeling came from where the bird's eyes should have been but the bird had no eyes and so I only felt empty inside but the emptiness fluttered in my chest like a bird as if the emptiness wanted to leave me but couldn't because it was stuck. And once I felt the feeling a different thing came from a different time that had nothing to do with the bird or the wagon but only the hollow feeling and the feeling made me see the empty space between the driveway and the garage door. I saw the opening where the dog's snout should have been. And when I didn't see the dog's snout I looked behind me and I saw the car still running with the headlights shining and when I followed the headlights I saw my hand and the keys. And I could feel the heat of the asphalt coming through the thin soles of my shoes even though the sun was almost gone and there was only twilight. And once I saw the car the headlight and the keys and once I saw that the dog that was always there was not there I was scared that everyone I had come to see was gone and those things that surrounded everyone I had come to see were gone too. And because there was nothing else to see I could suddenly feel and I remembered the feeling of being empty but before I could really feel the feeling of being empty I heard myself jingle the keys in my hands and I saw myself walk up the path to the door of the house that was not my house but my friend's house and when I rang the bell there was no answer. There was no dog and there was no answer and so I jumped over a bush and walked around to the side of the house where I jumped behind another bush and I pressed my face against the pane of the window and I looked in and where I had wanted to see a television lighting up a room there was nothing but darkness and I couldn't see the father in front of the television and when I strained my neck to look to the right where the light of the kitchen always was there was no mother in the light of the kitchen and there was no light and when I stopped pressing my face against the windowpane and when I came out of the bushes I looked up and when I felt the air and saw the strange gray color of the evening sky I thought that maybe this night was not just a humid summer night but a part of the world that had been emptied of everything including light and whoever had come to empty this part of the world had forgotten to evacuate me with the dogs and parents and I had been left behind in a strange fold of the universe with no other people but with only my car keys and my car and the strange gray light of the sky and when I stood still I heard suddenly a buzzing sound and when I looked out towards the empty street I could see the light of the streetlamp in front of the house fading and then turning bright again and because the buzzing grew stronger when the light grew stronger I thought that whatever had erased this part of the universe whatever force had taken my friend and her dog and everyone else in the neighborhood and had left me behind was now trying to shut out the light but the light didn't want to give up. The light didn't want to leave me alone in an abandoned corner of Bennington Drive outside on the lawn of a dead house. And because I was too scared to see if the streetlamp would win or lose I jumped into my car and turned on the radio and began driving and I could tell in all their talk that they had no idea that I had been left behind. They had no idea that I was alone in the fold after everyone else had been able to leave. And when I remembered these voices on the radio when I remembered hearing the two men talking I could remember how strongly I needed to know if I was alone and I stopped the car at a pay phone at the store that was always open that now was closed and I called the request line at the radio station and when I called I heard a machine answer and say *Thanks for calling WCNJ. Your call will be answered shortly.* And then I could hear the two men talking: *I do support that. I should not speak for Rob necessarily. But I do know that we both have a soft spot for animals. I love animals.* But when I tried to talk to them when I shouted *Hello Hello* I realized that they couldn't hear me that I was listening to the radio through the phone and before I could even hear the recording finish saying *Thanks for calling WCNJ your central Jersey station* for the second time I heard my quarter fall deeper into the phone and I heard another voice say *Please deposit another $.25 for the next three minutes* but I did not have another $.25 for the next three minutes so before I could try to say *Hello* again I only heard the drone of the dial tone. And that was the last thing I could remember. And once I finished remembering the two voices on the car radio I couldn't see anything except the light of the streetlamp coming through the window and falling on the dormitory wall and when I saw the street light falling on the wall I couldn't help but get out of bed and go to the window and make sure that the trees were still there and then I could only wonder where L— was because if I couldn't see the trees I couldn't see myself and I needed someone to see me so I could be myself and so I wanted L— to come to the window and look at me and see me so I could see the trees so I could come back to living in the world. But it was too late to find L—. It was too late to go out into the night across the cold grass of campus and wake her and make her look at me and so I could only stand there at my window and hope that I would look at the trees and they would suddenly look the way they used to look. That suddenly everything would look the same. But now when I stood at the window and looked at the trees I was there and not there like a ghost and so I could only see the things in the trees that were there and not there too and so I thought of L— and the grass and the dirt and I thought of how I felt now that I was standing at the window without really being there and when I thought some more about how it was possible that I could stand there and still not really be standing there at the window I thought about the cough medicine my mother made me take. The cough medicine with Codeine. I took the cough medicine with Codeine and then I floated down the stairs and I walked to my mother. I walked to my mother and I stood in front of her and I told her I wasn't like other boys. I was floating and I said *I'm sorry mother but I'm not like other boys* and she said *Of course you're not you're a girl* and then I saw the Codeine and the cough syrup go in the trash and I saw my mother sit down at the table and drink her tea and smile and everything I saw showed me that nothing had changed even though I had said something to my mother after taking the cough medicine. But everything had changed because the memory stayed and the mother kept the memory and because she kept the memory when she looked at her girl who was not like other boys she knew that if she laid a hand on her she knew if she laid a hand on her girl that her hand would go right through her girl because she wasn't really there anymore. Her girl wasn't there anymore so the mother didn't hug her and she didn't hit her. It would go right through her. She was not there. So the mother kept her boy. She kept her boy but looked the other way.

The RIVER

The next time I met L— it was a few days later in the afternoon after class and I could make my feet meet the pavement at the same time her feet met the pavement and when I looked over my shoulder I saw her shoulder—I saw the freckle coming out of the hole in her shirt from inside her coat and when I saw the skin of her shoulder with the freckle I felt like I knew how it would feel against my mouth and then I would look away at the trees and pretend I wasn't listening to our feet but I was careful always to be listening to the sound of L—'s feet so that our feet would fall on the pavement together. I was careful always to be listening.

I had a dream about you. I could hear the birds and hear L— talking too. *I had a dream that I couldn't find you and I was standing at the statue of Marcus Aurelius.* It was as if I could make the sounds of the creatures in the trees the music in L—'s words. *You said that you would come but you didn't come.* I could hear her louder than anything—louder than any voice in my head. *It was late. I thought I should walk to try to find you but it was hard for me to move. I could only walk in circles around the statue and so I waited for you but you never came.* When she spoke these sentences her voice was like a bird's. Soft and nervous.

They calmed me for a second—the words. They told me what to do and I could list the rules in my head. I had to protect L— from her own dreams and the way that I could protect her from her own dreams was to get everywhere on time. She wasn't ever to be alone waiting for me. I was here to make sure the dream would never ever be true. That was something I could do. I could stop the dream. It made me feel strong as if I could stop a train and I wasn't scared. She was my bird and I would protect her from her dreams.

I heard the birds and I could see the trees and I wanted to touch L— and I wanted to be the only thing strong enough to touch her. But the more I wanted to touch her the more I wondered if I could be stronger than the dream. And I thought if the dream was still following her then she could only hear her own footsteps falling and the birds in the trees. She could only wonder where I had gone and I wanted to make a little sound as if to say *Hello I'm still here* to see if she would turn my way and see my face and see that I was still here but I was too nervous and I worried that if I whistled I would only hear the sound of the birds in the trees and I would learn that the story of her dream was true and I would hear that I had disappeared. So I didn't whistle and I stopped listening to her feet falling on the pavement and I tried to stop listening to the birds in the trees.

But then suddenly I felt so quiet that I worried I had disappeared and I wanted to see if I had so I got the courage to whistle but I could never whistle very well so even though I tried to whistle the birds stayed loud and that's how I knew the dream was winning. My lips felt weak as if the air just fell through them and the weaker they felt the more I wanted to kiss L— but I was worried that kissing her would make me a part of her imagination because kissing her would be almost like becoming a part of her body and then I would just be a part of her and not myself anymore and so in a sense I would disappear into her and her dream would come true but still somehow I wanted to kiss her. I wanted to be close to her. I thought she could quiet the birds.

I kept trying to listen for our footsteps falling on the pavement together. But I was too scared to ask her if she could hear me whistle and I was too scared to ask her if she could hear my footsteps or if she found the birds too loud or if I could kiss her.

And then I felt L— grab my hand and when I felt her skin against my fingers I felt my face go hot and I looked down but I didn't miss noticing the sound of our feet together again. I didn't let the sound go. I wanted to be there. And even though I felt my face get hot I didn't let anything go and I squeezed her fingers tight and I didn't kiss her and I didn't listen to the birds anymore.

Lying in the grass with L— I could see the bridge in the air downriver and I could hear the car doors opening and closing behind us and sometimes wrapped in the wind I could hear the voices of two men but I couldn't tell what they were saying. And I could feel the skin of my face grow tight from the cold air and the tighter it grew the more I felt the bruise stretched by the skin around it but once we were in the grass I wasn't nervous about someone seeing us and I didn't worry about disappearing because I had stopped thinking about L—'s dream when I saw the bridge. I was just nervous about how we would get out of the grass without anyone seeing us.

I thought of a plan. To the right of us along the water there were some bushes and I thought we could crawl over to the bushes and stand up once we were behind them. Then we could walk in the direction from which we had just crawled and it would look as if we had just emerged from behind the bushes from down the river by the bridge then we could walk back along the bank and eventually we could just walk out straight to the road like two normal people walking who got lost along the river and once I figured out that plan I relaxed and didn't worry anymore and I felt quiet though I wondered if the stretched skin around the bruise would break the scab.

But I didn't worry. I just looked at the bridge in the sky and listened to the car doors and felt the dry grass scratch against my neck and when I saw and felt and heard everything I could I remembered how I felt when I wanted to kiss L—. I felt hollow. And as soon as I remembered the feeling I felt it again and I worried that the hollow feeling would make me want to leave so I closed my eyes. I knew it was the bridge and the river and everything else I saw around me that made me feel hollow when I thought about kissing L—. So I didn't want to see anything. I wanted to stay there and not see anything. And not leave L—. And I wanted to kiss L—.

And even though I knew I was in my body because when I opened my eyes I could see my hands moving in front of my face I felt outside of myself as though I were floating above both our bodies in the grass and I knew that if I wanted to be in my body again I would have to leave the place next to L—'s body and I would have to leave the river and sit in the chair at my desk in my room where I couldn't see the bridge in the sky and I couldn't see the river. I would have to be in my room where I could think about the bridge and the river as if they were imaginary places because now that the bridge and the river were real places I worried that I was a bad person. I worried that I was a bad person and the only thing I wanted to do was be in my imagination until dinner time so I could forget I was a bad person. So I could forget that I had gone to the river with L—. More than anything I wanted to be good.

But still I wasn't sure if I wanted to leave L—. I had promised myself not to let the dream win and I couldn't leave her alone by the river without letting the dream win. But I wasn't very sure that I wanted to stay with L— by the river either and when I knew that I didn't know where I wanted to be I could feel myself shake as if part of me was in my body and part of me was coming out of my body and floating away from the river so I put my hand on the bruise and even though that made me come back into my body it made me angry at L— for making me come to the river. It made me angry at L— for making me a bad person. But I had promised myself I wouldn't leave because I didn't want to leave L— and somehow coming to the river even though it made me feel like a bad person it also made me feel like I wouldn't ever disappear because now there was somebody who didn't want me to leave her. And for some reason it seemed better suddenly to be a bad person than to disappear.

And when I closed my eyes again L— leaned over and pulled on my ear and laughed so I opened my eyes and I tried to smile because I thought if she were laughing I should at least be smiling because if I were going to stay by the river it was important for L— not to know I felt like a bad person but when I tried to smile I could only hear the car doors opening and shutting behind us. I tried to distract myself and I thought to myself that L— looked like a little girl when she laughed. So I thought maybe I could pretend I was a little boy and together we were little kids lying in the grass along the river in the sun. And so I tried to think that but because it was almost dark and because it was almost winter I knew two little kids would not be lying in the grass along the river so it was difficult to pretend. But even so because L— looked like a sweet little girl when she laughed there was a part of me that thought it was all right to lie in the grass along the river with her because I knew that bad things weren't beautiful. Maybe lying along the river with L— was just something some people thought was bad but it wasn't really bad because bad things aren't beautiful and I knew L— was beautiful and as long as I could stop seeing the bridge in the distance and not hear the car doors slamming I could see that L— was beautiful and whenever I looked at her and saw that she was beautiful she smiled at me without me even saying anything and I would remember the part of the poem that went *I want to stop keeping my body like a teacup in a dust store* but even though I knew the poem wanted me to stay by the river and touch L— still I couldn't feel all good about it no matter how much I reasoned with myself and so I closed my eyes again. And when L— asked me what was wrong I said I could hear the car doors slamming and I was scared that the men would see us in the grass but L— said they wouldn't care. She said it was other people that would care. People who would never come down to the river but we didn't need to worry because those people never came to the river and if they did the grass was too tall to see us. And when she finished telling me that everything was ok I tried to act as if I believed her. I tried to act as if the bridge and the cars and the men didn't make me nervous because I didn't want her to know that there was anything that made me scared of being with her because I didn't want her to think I might leave her because suddenly now more than anything I wanted her to love me. I needed her to love me because suddenly I felt so lonely there in the grass by the river that I couldn't bear the thought of being alone and I knew from her dream that L— wanted to love somebody who would not leave her so I knew if I just stayed there in the grass next to her long enough I wouldn't be lonely and so I tried not to be scared.

And then she took her hand and made a circle around the bruise on my forehead and she didn't look at me but only at the bruise as if the bruise were not a part of me or as if I weren't there anymore but she were alone in the grass with the bruise like a strange rock she had found so I didn't say anything and L— didn't ask anything either. And though part of me wanted to tell her the story of the bruise there was part of me that knew she didn't want to hear the story of the bruise because already I could see she was trying to imagine the bruise separate from the rest of me so I could tell that she was hoping that the story of the bruise wasn't really a part of me though I didn't know yet why she didn't want the bruise to be a part of me. I just knew that I should be strong and not leave her at the river because I wanted her to love me and that's where I had to be if she were going to love me.

But I knew if I told her how I got the bruise it would bring us together in a real way but because she kept looking at the bruise as if it were not a real part of me—as if it weren't sitting there on my forehead but just lying on its own in the grass I could tell she was scared of it. And I thought somehow that it was her dream that made her scared of the bruise—I thought somehow that maybe her dream made her scared that the story of the bruise would also be the story of how I would leave her because I had already learned from stories in books that it was always the bruise with which somebody had come through the door that made that somebody always walk out the same door and not come back. But to tell the truth I was scared to tell her the story of the bruise not because I thought it would make me leave her but because I knew it would make me stay. So I wasn't sure if I wanted her to be the person who knew the story of the bruise because I wasn't sure if I could be strong enough to stay with her at the river.

And part of me thought it wasn't important to tell her the story of the bruise because she was so beautiful and I very much wanted to press my body against someone so beautiful but it seemed to me that the reason that she was so beautiful was partially because I could see in her eyes a little girl who was scared someone would leave her and this made her seem very real and I thought it would feel good to have my body close to someone who was so real and so beautiful and if I finally pressed my body against someone so real and so beautiful it would be as if I had listened to the poem. Maybe then my bruise would go away and there would be nothing about me to scare L— and I wouldn't have to tell her the story of my imagination and we could just press against each other by the river forever without being scared.

And even though I was too scared to touch her now I was lying in the grass next to her and I was lying close enough to her that when we breathed in at the same time I could feel our rib cages touching through our coats and if I didn't think about anything except our breathing the feeling of our coats pressing against one another felt good. And for a long time we just breathed next to each other like this and as long as we were breathing together it didn't seem as though we were different from one another and I liked L— again and I stopped being angry at her for taking me to the river and making me see that she was beautiful even though she refused to listen to the story of my bruise. And I wondered what it would feel like to have her touch my skin and I wondered if she wondered what it would feel like to touch my skin and all the wondering made my stomach feel light and everything felt warm around me.

But then L— turned on her side and I couldn't feel her against my coat anymore so I turned to see where she had gone only to see that she was still next to me with her head propped up on her arm and I thought she was maybe looking at me and when I thought she was looking at me I hoped that she was looking at me and thinking I was beautiful even though I had the bruise on my forehead but when I turned to look at her I saw that she wasn't looking at me at all but only into the distance over the grass and because she was looking at something so far away it was as if she too were suddenly very far away and I was glad suddenly that I hadn't asked her if she wondered about what it would be like to touch my skin because if I had I would have felt lonely when she suddenly started looking so far away and left me here alone with myself wondering if she would touch me.

But when I turned to look at her to see if she were looking at me even though she hadn't been looking at me she did turn suddenly to look at me but then she turned her eyes to the ground and bit the side of her lip and she didn't move so suddenly I wasn't sure if she wanted to be there with me and I felt lonely so I closed my eyes and when I did I could feel her hand come under my coat and then under my shirt and her hand was cold against my hot belly and it was strange and nice to feel the coldness of the grass and the river and the dirt against my belly though my wool coat was on and my shirt was on—still her hand had snuck in to touch my skin and it made me feel good for her to touch my skin because I thought maybe she thought that I was beautiful too and at that moment there was nothing I wanted more than for her to think I was beautiful so I relaxed a little and just let myself feel her hand against my skin and the more I felt her hand against my skin the more I felt my body grow tight because I was scared to move because I didn't want to do anything that would make her take her hand away. So we laid there like that for a very long time and I was careful not to say anything or to move and I just watched to make sure she wouldn't disappear.

But soon it was too tiring to be lying there so still and I just wanted to feel good with L—'s hand against my skin and not worry that she would move so part of me thought why shouldn't I feel good with her hand against my skin so suddenly I thought to stop letting myself think that I was a person separate from everything around me and I let myself think that I was a part of L—. I let myself imagine that my body was an extension of her hand and everything that we touched was a part of us and everything was beautiful and suddenly it was as if we were part of the landscape or a small part of me had become part of L— and I didn't worry so much anymore about the sounds of the cars or if L— would take her hand off of me.

And then she sat up and unbuttoned the bottom two buttons of my coat and she didn't look at my face but only at her hand and then she pulled the rest of my shirt out of my pants and she put her mouth to my belly twice gently and I could feel the heat of her mouth round against me with its wetness and I could feel the grass grow warm around my thighs and just when I felt so much in my body again I thought that I was a person and not part of everything that I saw around me so I was worried I would start to feel nervous again but L— pulled my shirt down just in time and she laid her head to rest on my belly and she looked up at me and then closed her eyes and held my hand in her two hands and my other hand was outspread in the grass away from us and I wanted to move that hand to touch the back of her neck but I couldn't but still I thought for a little bit that everything was a part of us.

The COLOR of STRAW

After I spent those hours in the grass by the river with L— I stopped thinking about the bridge and the men and the car doors slamming and L—'s dream and even the river itself as if they were real things but only an atmosphere I had entered once. A mood that took on the faded color of straw in the grass. So the next day whenever I thought about the time I spent with L— by the river it felt less like something that happened the day before than a strange dream that I had together with L— in a place that wasn't a place connected to any real world but more like a separate and foreign cell sprung from the giant amoeba that was school. And the bridge when I looked up and saw it rising in the distance was less of a bridge now and more the symbol for loneliness that it had always been but now when I saw it I felt a direct kind of loneliness that felt like the wind chafing my face and L— grabbing my hand and that hidden place along the river. It felt more like a loneliness that L— and I shared.

And I knew L— felt the loneliness too because she was a different person outside of the grass. Eating our tomato soup and grilled cheese sandwiches together during lunch we were both careful not to be too close to each other in case we might be tempted to touch each other but we never did. And as we talked she looked at me in the same way that she looked at Emily or Amanda or Daniel. It was as if nothing had ever happened between the two of us and I thought maybe the grass really had been a dream because Emily didn't look at me in the way that she did whenever she knew something happened to me and she always knew when something had happened to me. She and L— just talked about our literary theory class and how that morning we had discussed Kant's Third Critique and how it said that if something were beautiful it would be beautiful to anyone who ever saw it always even if they never saw it and as we talked I looked carefully at L—'s face again and wondered how I didn't think it was beautiful now but in the grass how I thought it was beautiful and how she must not really be beautiful because I would think she was beautiful every time I saw her always or maybe there was a way that I could not really see her now outside the grass because only if I really saw her would I know she was beautiful and somewhere she was visible and beautiful but I couldn't get to that place now and so I thought for the first time maybe the grass along the river was a real place where I saw things as they truly are and school wasn't.

So even though the grasses seemed like a dream I thought maybe they were a real place in the way that a dream is a real place for feelings and ideas and there in the dream of the grasses I could see that L— was really beautiful and I could feel a kind of loneliness creep up my shirt with L—'s hand because I thought she was beautiful and maybe that loneliness that crept up my shirt was a real loneliness that was mine and hers because I knew I was not supposed to think L— was beautiful even in the grasses but I was someone who could not stop thinking L— was beautiful and she was not someone who was supposed to creep her hand up my shirt even in the grass and though it seemed like a dream I thought maybe it was more real—the beauty and the loneliness I felt in the grass—because I felt them only when I was suspended in the imaginary space of the grass and everyone knows that the imaginary space of dreams is more real than the real space of the Sharpe Refectory and for that reason I could remember the dream of the grass very well even though I was back at school again eating a grilled cheese sandwich.

And after lunch the time in the grass seemed more real than ever because after Emily and Amanda and Daniel went on to their classes L— walked me over to Sayles Hall and asked me if I wanted to walk with her off-campus to her house tonight after dinner and I knew that L— wanted to be with me in the dream again and when she asked me I knew that I wanted to be in the dream again too so I said yes but I didn't touch her and I didn't smile and she didn't touch me and she didn't smile. We just looked at each other quickly and she turned and walked towards the green and sat on the grass and waited for me to finish with class.

The HOUSE

The smell of the river was so strong in the damp air that if I hadn't noticed coming through a door I might have thought we were still outside. The wind brought the smell through an open window that I didn't see at first because the house was dark. Floorboards creaked as we walked and each time they creaked I tried to walk more softly as if there were someone I might wake in the house. But I knew that we were alone. L— told me so. There was no one to wake. Still there was something about going up the unlit stairs through a dark corridor that made me feel as though there might be someone asleep behind one of the closed doors we passed. I had to be careful not to wake the person. I had to be careful not to let them see me enter L—'s room. I was careful in how I walked. I tried to walk quietly.

The only light was street light that filtered through the gauze curtains in her bedroom and reflected off the mirror of an old wardrobe. The street light lit us from behind and kept us more shadow than person but the mirror bounced us enough reflection to give us faces. Though I didn't like watching us together. I only looked once quickly.

She left me in the room alone for a few minutes and then I walked up to the mirror so that my nose nearly touched it. The only thing I saw was my own face. But just to make sure it was my own face I winked one eye and that eye winked back in the mirror and then I winked the other eye and that eye winked back too. And I tilted my head one way and then the other and the head in the mirror did the same. And the pupils in the eyes in the mirror looked back at me as hard as I had looked at them. It was my head. And there was no one else standing behind me and no one standing in front of me. I was with myself alone. There were just my eyes wide and tired and my cheeks red from walking and my hair covering the bruise and L— walking back in the door. And when I saw that L— was in the mirror behind me and I turned around and saw her in real life behind me I knew that I was doing what the bruise needed me to do and if I kept doing it maybe it would go away.

Once L— came back into the room and the door was closed I could hear that the house was quiet in the same way that all empty houses are quiet. Only an occasional crack or squeak—one that had nothing to do with a person moving but only with the house settling into itself. The sound of the emptiness made me feel empty in an old familiar way but even though it was familiar the feeling was something I didn't want to feel so I listened for people outside the house but there was no one on the street. There was only the sound of the wind in the trees. I started to hope that someone would come home soon just to hear someone moving in the kitchen—the dishes clanking and the light touch of the silverware being put on the table—just to know that L— and I hadn't been left and forgotten. Just to know that we could be part of a real world too.

Because of the feeling I knew right away that this house was haunted not by ghosts but by the spirit of another house and when I realized that it was haunted I knew that L—'s house wasn't haunted by the spirit of another house but that I was haunted by the spirit of another house and the spirit was inside me but would only come out when I felt alone in houses. And even though I could watch myself feel the memory—even though I could say to myself *M— you are having memories of another house*—the memory of the feeling of this other empty house was so strong in me I couldn't let go of it even though I could see it and name it I could only watch myself swim in it and I forgot that L— was not also haunted by the feeling and when I thought that she was feeling exactly what I was feeling I became more frightened because I thought she was stuck here too and wouldn't be able to help me get out. We would just fall into a particular kind of loneliness together. One that I had only ever felt in houses but never felt at school.

But then L— grabbed my hand and smiled and I realized she wasn't spooked by the house so I wasn't so frightened and I held onto her. And then she placed her hand against my cheek and there was something about the feeling of her hand against my cheek that made me feel protected and something inside me fell open and when I felt it fall open I could only bury my face in L—'s neck. There the loneliness of the house disappeared and when she kissed my skin I just felt the things that were there to feel instead of the things that weren't there and then the ghost of the house didn't so much seem to be in the room with us. I thought about how her lips felt against my neck and how the back of her neck felt against the palm of my hand and how her hair fell over the back of my hand and I thought if I kept thinking of these things I wouldn't fall back into the feeling of a house that wasn't there anymore. I could just be with L— and feel alive.

And something about the memory of the house made me not want to move away from L—. I felt like a small child and I wanted to stay close to her protected by her body but I was scared for her to know how I felt because it seemed that feeling like a small child was the wrong thing to be feeling so I didn't say anything to her. I just tried to keep my mouth close to hers and my hands on her body.

And then we sat down on the bed and though she had just put her lips on my neck as we were standing now sitting next to each other with our hands at our sides she seemed strange to me and it seemed strange to move my hands towards her again and it felt like it would be very difficult to touch each other again and I could tell L— was feeling the same way because she was biting the side of her lower lip and looking at the floor and I wanted to help her but there was nothing I could do with my body except talk and so I asked her if she liked living so far from campus and she said she did because she was a very private person and she felt like she could come home after school and she could live like a real person in a real house and no one would watch the way she was living. She could just live. And though I didn't understand how she thought that she could live in a real way without any friends down the hall to witness that she was living in a real way I didn't want L— to feel any stranger than she already did sitting next to me on her bed biting her lip so I answered carefully and I only said *Oh.* And then afterwards I thought about what L— said and it scared me because I realized L— was someone who didn't want to be a part of school because she didn't want anyone to look at her and I thought if I connected myself to someone who didn't want to become part of school I would stop being a part of school and no one would look at me any more and I would just live in my imagination with L— but I knew that if I wanted to live in the real world with real people I had to be part of more than just my imagination and so I never wanted to live anywhere where no one real could look at me and help make me real.

And then L— asked me why I still lived on campus when I could live in my own apartment in town and I told her that I didn't ever want to feel lonely and I felt strange when I said the words because I hadn't been thinking them and so I tried to understand what made me say the words and when I looked around to see I saw that the window was open and there was a breeze bringing in the smell of the river and I knew then it was the river that made me say the word *lonely.* And then L— asked me what it was that would make me feel lonely if I didn't live on campus and I wanted to say that it was the river but I was scared that if I told her that it was the river that made me feel lonely she would think that being with her made me feel lonely because to be with her I had to be by the river but the truth was that even though the river made me feel lonely even when I was with L— the way I felt lonely when I was with L— was different than the way I felt lonely when I was by myself. The difference in the way that I felt lonely with L— as opposed to the way I felt lonely when I was by myself was that I felt when I was with L— like we were lonely together. I felt like she and I were together and that didn't feel so lonely but that when we were together we weren't connected to anything else in the world anymore and that felt lonely and even though that scared me still I liked finally feeling together with someone in the way that I felt together with L— but I didn't know how to explain any of this to her so I said I always felt lonely when I was in a quiet house alone and although it wasn't exactly what I was thinking at the moment it was a sentence that was true so I hadn't lied to L— there was just too much to tell her to tell her the whole truth now and so I thought maybe someday I could tell her all of it.

And something changed in L— when I told her that I felt lonely when I was in a quiet house because she moved closer next to me and she grabbed my hand and held it in her hand and bit the side of her lip and stared at the floor. And I felt good when she grabbed my hand because for the first time I thought there was someone who didn't want me to be lonely and I felt grateful to L— and I wanted to be good to her and I asked her if we could lie down next to each other on her bed and she said *Ok* and we took our shoes off and I set them straight alongside each other next to her nightstand and then I set myself straight alongside her on her bed and together we stared at the ceiling as if we were staring at the stars and we stared together at the ceiling that could have been the stars for what must have been a very long time and I was close enough to L— that I could smell the sweetness of her skin and the sweetness of her sheets too and the sweetness of the sheets smelled like my grandma's home and so I wasn't scared. I just pretended I was visiting my grandma's house with a friend and suddenly I was so tired and I wanted to turn on my side and move close enough to L— so that I could fall asleep with my lips touching her neck but I couldn't. I couldn't move my body.

But I could move my arm so I grabbed her hand and I held it and I slept like that for what seemed like a very long time.

The GLASS of WATER

I dreamt that I was in a room—a large room with large windows—and outside the room it was night and there was nothing outside the room except the sky. The room I knew was a classroom although there was nothing in the room that let me know it was a classroom. There was no desk or chalkboard. And the few things that were in the room didn't seem to belong in a classroom. But I knew in the dream that I was standing in a classroom and I think I knew it was a classroom because the windows were so large.

I was at the window standing next to the nightstand on which there stood a lamp. It was the only light in the classroom. It was a small lamp. It was the kind of small lamp that belonged in a child's room—a lamp with a thick paper shade.

There were stars on the shade. The sky was dark. The lamp's light wasn't very strong.

Because I was standing next to a nightstand I naturally expected a bed to be standing there next to it or at least a mattress. But there was no bed and there was no mattress even though I expected there to be one. And I only expected there to be one because every time I had ever been next to a nightstand I had also been on or next to a bed or at least a mattress. So naturally I found standing next to a nightstand with no mattress very strange. I found it very strange and I said to myself in the dream *This is very strange.* And after I said it to myself I knew suddenly that the bruise had not only taken the trees and left only the sky but it had also taken the mattress. And once I knew this I was able to watch myself in the dream standing at the window. And once I was able to see myself in the dream I was also able to look around the room to see if there was a mattress and when I looked around I saw a mattress. I couldn't have seen it very well from where I stood near the window not knowing that I was in a dream but I saw it once I could watch myself in the dream. It was in one of the dark corners of the classroom where there was no window. The lamp left the corners of the room nearly dark.

I was looking out the window at the sky looking either for a tree in the field or my face on the glass. I couldn't see myself reflected in the glass of the window although I was next to the lamp and the lamp was lit and outside it was still very dark so I thought maybe I was looking for a tree in the field instead of my face in the glass. But I don't know if this is why I was staring out the window because the part of me that watched myself in the dream wasn't exactly the part of me that was in the dream staring out the window so I wasn't sure what the part of me that was in the dream was looking for. I wasn't sure if she was looking for the tree or my face. And I couldn't tell exactly what she was thinking because sometimes I was looking out of her eyes as she stood there at the window and sometimes I was only the dreamer watching her there. I only know that when I saw through her eyes I could only see the sky and no matter how hard I looked for my face in the glass of the window it wasn't there. The lamp was on and I was standing next to it and the night was dark so there was no reason why my face shouldn't have been there. But I didn't see it.

I was nervous that the bruise took the tree and my face like it took the mattress. But when in the dream I was the dreamer watching the dream I couldn't see if I had a face because I could only stand behind her and watch her stare out the window. I couldn't look for my face in the same way I had looked for a mattress. And when I was in the dream staring out the window I thought I was looking for a tree as much as I was looking for my face and so I must have thought that if the bruise gave me the tree back it would give me my face back too.

When I turned away from the window I the dreamer was now the same as I who was in the dream because I suddenly stopped seeing her and could see everything through her eyes and when I tried to touch her head I only saw my own hands in front of my face. I was glad that I finally knew that I had a face but I couldn't see it. I could only feel it.

I walked away from the window towards the center of the room to a chair and on the seat of the chair there was a wine glass filled with water. The water came very high nearly to the rim of the glass so that when I picked up the glass and held the glass but didn't drink from it I had to be very careful not to spill the water. As I was holding the glass carefully so as not to spill the water I began to wonder why this glass of water was in my dream and why I was holding it so carefully in the dream and although I was in the dream with the glass of water it was very difficult for me to know what it meant so I stood there holding the glass. And as I stood there with my glass wondering what it meant I heard a girl's voice coming from the mattress and even though I couldn't see the girl I said to myself *That's G—*. G— was speaking very rapidly so rapidly it was as if she were reciting something from memory as if it were a poem or something else she had memorized. But I didn't understand any of the words in her poem but I thought that since it was my dream I should change her words so that I could understand them but even though I thought this while I dreamt I still couldn't change anything. I still couldn't understand the words of the poem.

The sound of the words in G—'s poem made me nervous because they sounded wild and although I didn't know what the glass of water meant I knew I should be careful not to spill it and I worried that the waves the words sent into the air would be strong enough to make the water in the glass vibrate and spill and so I got angry at G— for causing such chaos and I said *Be quiet G—. You'll wake L—*. And I moved the glass of water closer to my chest knowing now suddenly that it was L— who was the glass of water and I knew this now not because I had understood anything but simply because I had said that L— was the glass of water.

I didn't want to spill her so I shouted to G— *Don't think I'm going to let you spill her*. I shouted it so loudly that I almost spilled L— myself and when I saw the water in the glass move I knew that I had to be careful not to get too angry or else I would hurt L—. G— didn't care that it was so easy to spill

L— and instead of keeping quiet she shouted back to me *Why don't you drink her M—?* And before I could even think about what to say I whispered carefully *Because she shouldn't be inside me.* And before I could even understand what I had just said G— shouted *She already is.* But when I looked into the glass I saw that the water was still there and so I didn't know what G— meant and she didn't say anything more to help me understand. She just recited more poems that I didn't understand and although the words didn't make any sense to me the sound of them made me thirsty and I was tempted to drink from the glass of water but I didn't want L— inside me because I didn't want anything that G— had said to be true.

But then I thought if I didn't drink the glass of water I could become very weak and I could pass out and then G— could take the glass of water and do whatever she wanted with it. But it was my glass of water so why should she touch it. So I said to myself *Drink* and when I said this to myself I lifted the glass to my mouth and just as I was about to press the glass to my lips I saw my face floating in the water and when I saw my face floating in the water my hand shook and the water spilled and before I could see if my face was still in the water now that the water was on the floor I woke up and I felt the bruise stronger than before.

I thought if I could only fall asleep again and dream my dream again and drink the water before I spilled it then I would be strong enough to move my body closer to L—'s and I would be able to sleep while touching her and if I could only sleep and touch her at the same time I knew that in the dream I would be able to drink the water and if I could only drink the water I would be able to get rid of the bruise. But the feeling of the bruise made me feel very awake and I was too awake to fall asleep as if it were trying to keep me from myself and keep me away from L— at the same time and so I could only lie on my side watching the breath come gently in and out of L—'s nose as she slept peacefully next to me.

The SLEEPERS

The treetops entering the frame in the bottom right-hand corner of the window and the clouds moving across the glass from the top left-hand corner and the blue the gentle morning blue of the morning sky as the background. I thought about where exactly I would make the cloud stop to make the window into a very good painting. It had to be near the top left corner where the cloud first entered—the place where the eye falls first. A good painting begins there my professor said. That's where I would stop the cloud.

Somewhere a metal door squeaked as it opened and quickly slammed shut. It opened again and the voice of a woman called out *Don't forget to go by the post office* and then a man called back *I won't* and then a car door slammed and an engine started shifted gears and faded slowly into distance. The metal door fell shut again. Birds chirped and the treetops were still for a moment in the bottom of the window frame and another cloud moved slowly through the sky across the glass. L—'s face was soft with sleep. Her body curled facing me the breath gentle and steady. Her hand was on my hip and I thought to myself *He with his palm on the hip of the wife and she with her palm on the hip of the husband.* Was I the husband or the wife? A lock of hair fell over her cheek. She was asleep. I made more paintings in the window.

Then outside there was laughter in the distance. And as the laughter came close below the window it stopped being soft and seemed to echo in the room with us. And then a boy said *What was I supposed to do? She saw me take it.* A plane came into the window frame and traced a vector from just below the clouds to just above the trees. *All the space was activated* my professor said. I was a good painter. And the boys were still laughing in the room. L— kept her hand on my hip. One shouted *You idiot.* And then the voices moved away and left us alone. I was a private painter. A bus screeched to a stop. The voices of the boys fell into a cave and disappeared.

And then everything was very quiet. L— turned onto her back still asleep and her hand fell from my hip. Nothing happened for several minutes. Then footsteps. *Hello John. Hello. How are you? Good. Good. Say hello to the Mrs. Will do.* The footsteps faded. Who was John? Who was the Mrs.? In the window there were only the treetops against a cloudless blue. The weather had deactivated the space. There were no more good pictures. Only endless sky. Who the husband? Who the wife? I was the painter watching my paintings fall apart.

I turned on my side. There were no more invisible paintings to make. Only the girl to kiss. I looked at her closely like I had never done before. I could see each eyelash brushing the tops of her cheeks and the faint freckles. The light one at the edge of her bottom lip almost camouflaged by the red flesh and the almost invisible freckles on her forehead and nose—ones I had never seen before. I looked at her very carefully so that she would become my picture. I was her painter and she didn't stir. A good model. And then I remembered why I came to look at her. Her lips. Lips like what? I tried to remember all the lips in all the poems:

> *Lips like roses. Like sugar. Like daffodils or daisies or blue phlox. Like roses of the world that lie unfurled. Lips like petunias or azaleas or antelopes or myrtle. Lips sweeter than Victorian box. Softer than vermilion dusk or velvet spray. L—'s sweet lips. The boring lips of boring poems. No. No boring lips for L—. Lips like a river. Like a river where at the bottom there's a rose and in the rose there's another river and in that river another rose. Yes. Those lips. Lips like a bed of cotton and shadow where the flesh is grass where the flesh is not an empty house. Lips like wet river. Yes. Like wet river. But not like coral or caterpillars or rotting logs or sleeping fish. And not like curtains or luggage or shoes slick with algae. No seaweed lips or lobster lips. No lips smacking like a banker's. No butterfly or bellybutton or broken sidewalk lips. No lips like Styrofoam or industry. Or lips like a zipper holding back sparrows. But lips like a river with a wound in it. A wound so deep it's filled with more river. A river so deep that the wound is nothing but river. Lips like shadows along a wounded river.*

And when I thought about her lips as wounds I thought suddenly if I kissed L— she would understand me and so it was easy that second to kiss her and when I pressed my lips to hers they didn't feel wounded but were soft and didn't stir and so I kissed them again. Again they didn't stir. And when they didn't stir again I wasn't afraid any more. They seemed my lips to kiss. So I kissed them again and then once again and then I wished they would kiss me back. And so I moved my bottom lip just below L—'s bottom lip and I brushed my lip upwards against hers and then both her lips stirred though L— barely moved and she did not open her eyes and before I knew it both her lips were kissing my bottom lip and everything in the room and the street was quiet except for our breathing and the quiet sounds of our kissing and the quiet kissing echoing in the quiet of the morning world made me realize that the poem had worked. As long as I could fall into the right river.

And part of the reason it had felt so good to fall was that falling into L—'s lips was like falling into the peacefulness of her sleep so that nothing around us was as real as the dream of us. I was drunk on the warm sweetness of her skin and when I pressed my cheek against her cheek I could only pull myself on top of her and match each of my limbs to hers and press into her like a stone tower tired of standing hoping to fall and disappear with perfect symmetry to perfect rest in its own reflection pool.

And I did fall into her and when I did L— turned me over onto my back and I was safe under the weight of her body and she kissed my face and neck and she pushed my arms down and the more she pushed me down the more I trusted that she wouldn't let anything in to hurt me or remind me that I was lonely and for a little while I forgot about everything. I didn't worry about the river or the bridge or the men in their cars or what Emily would think or if I would ever learn how to write a story where something happened or if the face in the mirror really was my face or if I could tell someone the story of my imagination or if there would ever be enough sentences in the world for someone to know all the thoughts in my head or if the bruise would ever go away. I forgot about the house and the dream and the glass of water. I just let L— kiss me.

But even though I was safe and hidden under her body a feeling of something that wasn't there in the room came over me and I remembered the heat of a certain day. I remembered that it had been around noon that day. The sun couldn't have been any stronger. And when I could feel that day again I kissed L— hard on the mouth and tried to keep the feeling of that day away. The sun was so strong. I wanted to be lost under her body but the sun was strong in the open part of the yard—everything seemed to disappear into its whiteness. I felt covered in it. Trapped alone in a shroud of light and heat though she was on top of me. And even though I dug my fingers into her shoulders and clasped the back of her neck still I found myself suddenly under the large pine cooling off in the darkness and though the branches surrounded me and kept me cool they made me feel trapped and alone again no matter how hard L— kissed me.

But still I didn't want to be alone so I took my shirt off and I took L—'s shirt off and I could feel her skin against mine and for a little while I didn't feel alone. But then I opened my eyes and I saw the sun coming in strong through the curtains. I wasn't allowed in the pool alone. I wasn't allowed to swim alone. Even though it was so hot in the room. I might drown my mother said. And then L— unbuttoned my pants and her fingers slipped inside me. I couldn't stand the sun any longer and soon all I felt was the water around me. I felt the water so much that I stopped feeling myself. I wasn't myself anymore.

I couldn't get close enough to her. She couldn't come deep enough inside me. I wanted to be the water and so I breathed it in. I forgot who I was. I kept pushing myself into her but I couldn't get any closer to her. She couldn't come inside me. I wanted to feel her in my mouth but I started to breathe and the chlorine burned me. I was choking. And then I was bent and hung over the aluminum wall and the water came out of me. I saw it come out of me. Her arms were tiny. There was not enough of her to touch me. I was breathing heavy when she collapsed onto me and I buried my face in her neck and kissed her softly and on her skin I smelled the grass and the river and I felt my heart beating through to her but still it was as if she couldn't touch me enough. And then she turned away from me on the bed and bit her lip and sat up and stared at the floor sighing once deeply. She stood up and put her shirt back on and she walked out of the room down the stairs and didn't look at me any more that day but only looked at the floor and sometimes bit the side of her lip and as we ate breakfast quietly together it was as if we had never fallen asleep together or even looked at each other and though I kept looking at her in the kitchen as we ate quietly she didn't look back at me once and I knew then that L— wouldn't be able to love me but more than anything I wanted L— to be able to love me because I thought if L— loved me I wouldn't have to be unreal anymore. If she could just look at me and be inside me the loneliness of the house could disappear and the bruise could go away forever.

The DIRT

The next time I met L— I kept walking. I didn't stop when we reached her house and she didn't say anything when I didn't stop. She just followed me. And if there hadn't been a river I would have kept walking and maybe she would have still followed me but there was a river and when I reached it there was nowhere else to go. So when I found myself knee deep in the grass I sat down and L— sat down too. But I was careful. I had to be careful. I was careful not to let L— touch me.

And I was careful to notice everything that was there around us in the grass. A bird hopped in the thick of a bush. The wind rippled across the water. It crept up my coat. And the dirt was cold and soft pressing against my palms as I leaned back in the grass. I raised my head up. The clouds moved fast bright against the blue of the sky. A car door slammed and a few deep voices drifted. And when I turned my head around I could see the bridge. And when I looked at L— she looked over my shoulder at the bridge. And the two of us were almost looking at each other sitting there on the damp dirt. On the dry straw of the grass in the cold coming off the river. And I didn't see anything or feel anything that wasn't there.

And I thought if we didn't move I could stay with her. There would just be the bird and the clouds and her gaze falling past me over my shoulder into the distance. No trees. No house. No body of mine falling into a sea of memory. And it stayed like that for a few minutes. But then she looked at me.

And when she looked at me she moved closer to me. And even though she didn't move close enough to touch me my body shook. My body shook and I looked down at the ground. But when I saw the shadow of her arm moving towards me across the grass and then moving across the dirt I looked up. I looked up and I grabbed her arm in my hand. I stopped her. She couldn't touch me. But I did it carefully. I didn't want her to know. I didn't want her to notice. I didn't want her to know she wasn't touching me. I came to my knees in the dirt. I was on my knees in the dirt right in front of her. And before she noticed I pressed my mouth hard against hers.

I pressed my mouth against her mouth and it felt as if we had no lips. Just the edges of our mouths rough and open against each other. Our teeth clashing. It felt hard and cold as if it weren't kissing but only our skulls pushing into each other. Our bones as cold as the water and the dirt. But I didn't want to stop. I was winning. She wasn't touching me. And then I pushed her down on the ground and we kept our mouths pushing against each other. And I slipped one hand under her coat. I slipped one hand under her coat and with the other hand I held her hands together and pressed them into the dirt behind her head. She couldn't touch me and the more she couldn't touch me the more I touched her. I pushed my hand across the skin of her stomach and I felt the skin change. I felt it grow rough and cold under my fingers. I didn't like the way it felt but I didn't want to stop. She couldn't touch me. And I moved my hand further and further down her belly. And I pushed two fingers between the fat of her belly and the tight edge of her pants. I got my fingers in her pants and she felt warm there. She felt warm and soft and I pushed further. I felt the edge of her panties and I got one finger in there. I got one finger in there and I felt something that made me scared to feel. Something warmer and softer. I felt it and I pulled away. I felt it and sat up. I pulled my finger out of her pants. I stopped. I let her go. I didn't touch her. I couldn't touch her. I didn't want to touch her. I had touched her. She was lying in the dirt. She was staring at me. I wasn't bad I said. I didn't want to be bad. Maybe I was a bad person. I said that. I said that and I said I was sorry. I kissed her on the lips softly and I didn't say anything after that. I sat there and I didn't say anything and she didn't say anything either before or after that.

The BRUISE

When I entered the apartment I entered into an unlit corridor the end of which opened into a slate blue room barely lit by a single lamp. The back wall of the room was a row of windows and the first thing I saw was G— sitting in one of the windows with one leg in the room and the other hanging outside of it. I could see the night sky above the city behind her. No one had heard me come in because there was music playing and everyone was talking loudly so I stood in the hall quietly looking at G—'s torso pressing against the glass of the half-closed window. She would have had to duck under the window in order to fall out. I thought that to myself because I was worried she could fall out. But I thought about how she was sitting and I thought since the window was partially closed she would be ok. She would be ok as long as she didn't put any other part of her body on the other side of the glass.

I didn't want her to hurt herself but then I started thinking so much about whether or not she could actually fall out the window that I started imagining her falling out the window over and over again. I imagined it so much that it made me think I shouldn't look at her anymore because maybe my thoughts would make her fall out the window and I didn't want to be a bad person who made a girl fall out the window. So then I stopped looking at her. I didn't look at her and I thought to myself *I just wanted to see L—*.

And when I started looking around the room I saw Nate sitting on a couch that was set perpendicular to the windows. He was holding a cigarette in the air with one hand and aiming a toy gun at G— with the other and he kept saying *Bang Bang Bang* and I wondered why he wanted to shoot G— and if G— was just a person that made everyone want to hurt her. There were two boys who I didn't know laughing at Nate for shooting G— and G— was laughing too every time Nate shot her and I thought maybe if G— was laughing it wasn't so bad that Nate wanted to shoot her. Maybe G— was the kind of person that wanted to be shot.

After I stopped watching Nate shoot G— I noticed that no one in the room looked right. Nate had put heavy black lines around his eyes and had painted his lips and so even though he was wearing the kind of T-shirt a boy should wear and the kind of shoes a boy should wear his face made him not look the way a boy should look. And the two boys who I didn't know didn't look right either. One of them was wearing a skirt even though he had a beard and the other one—even though he was dressed in boys' clothes—put his one arm on his hip in a V-shape while he held a glass in the other. Somehow the way he put his arm on his hip made him not look like a boy even though he was skinny and wearing clothes like a boy.

And then closer to me against the wall across from the couch were two girls who I didn't know leaning against the wall very close to one another and talking and they were both wearing men's suits and even though they were both wearing men's suits they were the kind of girls who had small angelic faces with little doll lips so even though they were wearing men's clothes they looked like girls wearing men's clothes and they too had painted lips. And that was the strange thing about the party. No one looked like a boy or a girl in the right way except for G— who looked like a girl and Nate wanted to shoot her and I kept imagining her falling out the window.

I was scared to walk into the party but just as I was thinking of turning around and walking out of the apartment Amanda came into the darkness and when she found me there on her way to the bathroom she asked me what I was doing and I said I had come looking for L— but Amanda said L— wasn't at the party yet. Amanda's eyes were a little droopy and she seemed to be half asleep. She was drinking whiskey from a glass and I think she didn't want to fall any more asleep because instead of drinking the rest of the whiskey in the glass she gave me the glass without saying anything and then she went into the bathroom and I stood alone in the dark holding the glass and thinking about drinking from it. When she came out of the bathroom back into the corridor we stood there in the dark together and that's when I started to drink the whiskey.

It wasn't long before I started to feel a warmth spread across my body and I could feel my eyes becoming droopy and then it seemed like there were all these feelings inside me that were heavy and I needed to talk about them. They came out of my mouth like gusts of air through the leaden muscles of my face. And I found myself saying things to Amanda like *The river was put here just for us Amanda* and no matter what I said it was as though Amanda knew exactly what I was talking about and she would say things to me like *I know. I know. It really was.* And soon I realized that it was the whiskey that was making us finally tell each other the truth and it made me have a special affection for the whiskey and soon we found ourselves another empty glass and so now we each filled up our own glass with whiskey. I kept telling Amanda how much I liked the bridge above the river and the seats in the library and the food in the dining hall and how much I liked to be with everyone who was at the party even if we never spoke a word to each other and that's when I knew I never wanted to leave school. And as I was talking to Amanda I was realizing that I was telling her everything that I liked so much about being at school but that I hadn't yet mentioned L— and something stopped me from telling her about how much I liked L— and when I stopped myself from telling Amanda how much I liked L— I looked around the room and I saw her.

She was sitting on the couch next to Nate laughing and I wondered how she got past us in the corridor but then I looked around and noticed that we weren't in the corridor anymore. We were on the floor slumped against the wall where the girls in suits had been earlier. And then I looked at L— until she looked over at me and when she looked over at me I lifted my glass and smiled at her and I could feel how heavy my glass and lips were from the whiskey and she looked at me and laughed but then turned to Nate and whispered something in his ear and he looked at me then too and he laughed and pointed his gun at me and said *Bang Bang Bang*. It made me wonder if L— told him to shoot me. And even though I was scared when he did shoot me I for some reason said *I'm dead* without thinking and I said it in this way that sounded like I wasn't scared of being dead and then I wondered if I really wasn't worried about L— telling Nate to shoot me or if the whiskey just made me act like I wasn't scared.

It must have only been a short time later that Amanda and I were sitting at a kitchen table with several empty glasses in front of us. I was next to Amanda and L— was across from us and she smiled at us a few times and I wasn't sure if she was mad at me or if she just didn't want anyone to know that I had ever slept in her bed but she wasn't saying anything to me. And then G— suddenly came over and sat next to her and started talking with her which I thought was strange but I couldn't say anything.

Everyone else who I had watched was now sitting with us too. Both of the girls in suits were resting on their elbows and their faces were lit by the bulb that hung above the table from a thick wire. Their faces were lit but their heads were in the dark. L— was turned to G— so her face was mostly darkened but sometimes she would move in closer to the table and then her whole head was lit too and then G— sometimes moved back from the table deeper into the chair and then her face disappeared. Nate looked like he could fall asleep but he kept talking to the boys who sometimes lifted their heads without opening their eyes much and they looked at one another and laughed and then rested their heads back on their folded arms.

And everyone sat around tired like this but talking until Nate finally shouted *Truth or Dare* and the two girls in suits got excited and shouted *Dare.* The boys laughed. G— and L— looked at each other. Amanda and I said nothing.

Everything was floating a little bit and Amanda pushed another filled glass towards me as if she knew we would need it to get through the game. It was Nate who made the first dare and he asked the hairy boy in the skirt to kiss the boy with pink hair and the hairy boy did. I couldn't look. I stared at the table and I was glad I was drunk because everything stayed unreal like in a dream. And then the boy with the pink hair made the next dare and he dared the one girl in the suit to take off the other girl's shirt and lick her from the belly button up to her lips and then to kiss her on the mouth and she had to put her tongue in the other girl's mouth. That was the dare. And I didn't want to watch it happen but I couldn't say so and when everyone watched I didn't watch. I looked at them so no one knew I wasn't watching but I let my eyes glaze over.

And while this was happening I saw the guy with the pink hair playing with the gun. I think that's what gave the girls in the suits the idea. I certainly didn't. I was quiet and looking down with my jacket buttoned up all the way to my neck. But after the one was done licking the other's belly the pink haired guy who looked like an evil girl clown was waving the gun around and he pointed it at G—. And right when the boy clown who looked like a girl pointed the gun at G— the girl who just finished licking the other girl got a glint in her eye. Then she looked at G— and said *I dare you to have someone fuck you with that toy gun. I dare you to get fucked with that toy gun while we watch.* And the way she said it was strange because the words themselves seemed so angry but she said them through her angelic little lips with a half-smile across her face. And G— without even thinking for a moment said *Ok* and looked at me and said *I want M— to fuck me with the gun* and I said without even thinking *I better go wash my hands* and then G— said *You might want to wash the gun too.* And L— laughed which made me think maybe L— was a bad person but I nodded at G—'s request and I could feel everyone in the room get excited and I thought that they were all bad people because it was bad if I fucked G— with the gun. But maybe they didn't know about the cuts on her thighs.

And when the boy clown gave me the gun I left the kitchen without saying anything. I went out of the kitchen into the living room and into the dark corridor where I didn't turn into the bathroom to wash my hands and I went out into the hallway and down the stairs and out of the building and I dropped the toy gun in the sewer. The streets were empty and I was scared. But there was no way I would go back inside.

I looked up and I saw streetlights and I could see the light bulb hanging in the kitchen through the blinds and everyone's shadow was moving around getting ready for me to come back in the kitchen. I waited a little outside the building hoping that L— would know that I wouldn't want to do the dare and that she would know somehow that I had left and that she would come looking for me before anyone else knew that something was wrong. But she didn't come. And then I started to get worried that someone else would come looking for me and I didn't want to have to explain why I left so I started walking down the road even though I was scared to walk back to campus alone this late at night.

At first I wasn't scared because I could hear things that made it sound like people were around. I could hear a dog barking in the distance and then I heard someone call *Come here boy—Come inside* and then I heard a screen door slam and the dog stopped barking. And then I passed a little bar that was lit up in red neon and there were still a bunch of cars parked outside and I could hear voices and music playing inside. Everything around the bar sounded happy so I wasn't so scared and I wished there were a bar on every corner until I got back to school.

And once the road got a little desolate it never seemed too desolate because every now and then a car would come up the road and eventually end up behind me. And when I walked to the side of the road to let it pass it always passed me without anyone inside bothering me. But it was a little bit scary every time a car passed because on that stretch of road it was dark and I couldn't see any houses. So I was scared every time a car passed because I was worried someone in the car would bother me and no one else could see me to help me. But then when the car passed without giving me any trouble I would feel glad that I had just seen people. I liked it when the car passed and I could hear everyone in the car talking to each other and having a good time. And then I would wish I was in the car with those people and not alone on the dark street.

But then after about ten minutes it seemed that the cars stopped coming and I got to a spot along the road where there were lots of thick trees. And suddenly I could hear two guys talking loudly and laughing somewhere inside the trees. And then I heard one of them say *Come on—Let's go ask him.* And then I heard them laugh loudly and the way they laughed made me scared. It wasn't like the laughter of the people in the bar or in the cars that passed. It was different. It was a secretive laugh like they were laughing at what they said because what they said was different than what they meant. So when I heard them laugh I got scared of course. And right after I heard them laugh I heard their feet walking across gravel somewhere inside the trees behind me.

And at first when I turned to look over my shoulder I didn't see anything. I just heard them somewhere off the road. But then after a few seconds I saw them. They had reached the road from a driveway hidden somewhere inside the trees. But it must not have been too hidden because they had seen me and now they were coming to ask me something. There were two of them and they had beards and I could tell they were older than I was but not too much older. They were carrying beer bottles in their hands. And when they hit the road they didn't say anything. I didn't hear them say anything. I just heard their footsteps walking quickly behind me. And soon they seemed to be getting closer. But I was too scared at that point to look back. And I started walking as fast as I could. And I could feel my heart start to beat faster. It seemed no matter how fast I was walking their feet were right behind me. For a second I thought about running but I didn't want them to think I was scared of them. And I didn't know where I could run to. I was still a few blocks from campus. And before I knew it I could smell beer and suddenly one of them jumped right in front of me. His face came really close to mine so close that I stopped walking so that I wouldn't smash my face into his. I could see how the skin on his lips was peeling and how he had a broken front tooth and a moustache stained from cigarettes and I could really smell the beer now. And when he finished looking me hard in the eyes he said *Hey man—Don't walk so fast. We were just wondering if you could help us out with some beer money. You look like a generous guy.* And when he finished speaking he started to laugh. He lifted his head up and I could see the streetlight shining into his eyes. It made him look for a second not like a person because the light washed away the depth of his eyes. For a second he looked soulless cackling there in the streetlight.

And as the guy in front of me was laughing the guy I couldn't see but who I had felt standing right behind me the whole time pulled my arms behind my back and grabbed the wallet out of my back pocket. And then the one in front of me said *Gee you sure are a pretty boy*. And then they both started laughing. And then I felt the one behind me let my arms go and then for a second I thought *That wasn't so bad* and I felt like everything was going to be ok. But then the one in front of me said *You're a little too pretty for a boy. I know what would toughen your look up a little.* And at first he smiled and cupped my cheek with his hand but then right when he stopped touching my face I saw the skin around his eyes tense up and he pulled his other arm back and swung. And before the bottle hit me in my forehead I remember I could see how tight the muscles in his face were and I remember I could see a sudden anger in his eyes. I don't remember how it felt when the bottle hit me. I don't know if they laughed at me when I hit the ground or if they got scared and ran. The only thing I remember after that was Amanda standing above me as I lay on the road and she called out to L— —who was somewhere behind us—I heard Amanda call out to L— *Oh my God—Oh my God—Oh my God.* And I felt my head aching and I felt the asphalt against my hands. And when I put my hand to my forehead and pulled my hand away and looked at it I could see the blood all over my hand. But I didn't feel sick. I was too tired to feel sick. I just waited for L— to reach my side. And when she did I said *It's bigger than before—the bruise is bigger.* And she didn't say anything. She just stood over me with her hand covering her mouth.

The PARABLE of The BRUISE

It took me several months after L— stopped talking to me to understand what about the bruise made it impossible for her to see me anymore but soon enough I realized that that was the problem: the bruise made it impossible for L— to *see* me and so she couldn't be with me anymore. And even though this fact made me lonely—lonelier than I had ever been—I slowly was able to understand what about the bruise made it impossible for L— to see me anymore because after L— left me I used everything I knew about L— and everything I ever heard anyone else say they knew about L— to write in my imagination the story of her imagination and once I knew the story of L—'s imagination I understood too that L— didn't leave me but rather that she left the bruise. And I began to understand the story of L—'s imagination not because she was ever able to tell me the story of her imagination but because I had listened carefully to the things she had told me as she told me them and even though at the time that she told me them I didn't understand exactly how the things she told me made the story of her imagination now that I knew that the bruise was difficult for her to look at in hindsight I could take L—'s words and write the story of her imagination and understand her better than anyone had ever understood her or might ever understand her even though she refused to ever see me again or maybe exactly because she refused to ever see me again and so I became the person who loved L— most in the world after she left me because I knew it was the person who could understand the story of a person's imagination best who loved a person most but even though now I was the person in the world who loved her most I was the person she could see least so all I could do was write the story of her imagination for myself and here is what I wrote:

Long before the bruise had fallen onto my forehead it had fallen into L—'s eyes so that already when she was a little girl there was a shadow that eclipsed her gaze and made the things around her not look like the things themselves but like bruised things. And the reason the bruise had first fallen into L—'s eyes when she was a little girl was because she had been forced to watch her mother die and more than anything when she was a girl L— had not wanted her mother to die. So L— had forced herself to watch her mother die because she thought if she looked at her mother dying long enough her mother would stop dying because each time L— looked at her mother as she was dying L— felt the pain as if it was her own pain and so L— thought that the pain was moving from her mother's body into her own eyes and if L— could just look at her mother's pain long enough she could take her mother's pain away and her mother would not die if only L— could take the pain away from her mother and hold it in her own eyes.

So L— already when she was a little girl was left with a dead mother and the shadow of the bruise in her eyes and this made her hate looking at anyone for very long because the shadow in her eyes when she looked at someone only made her worry that the person would die and leave her with only more pain and if there was anything in the world she didn't want it was another dead body and someone else's pain in her eyes. And so even though looking at the trees with me one night made her want to look at me more because she too liked the fact that we both looked at the trees at night to help us see how blue the black sky really was she could not look at me without looking through the shadow of her bruise and the shadow of her bruise could only remind her not to look at any one. And so the part of her that wanted to look at me was trapped behind the shadow of her bruise and when she did finally look at me she could only look at me through the shadow of her bruise and when she did finally look she saw my own bruise and she could only think it was something that she would be forced to carry and so the few times that she let herself look at me she clasped her own head and turned the other way. And the more L— turned away the more I wanted her to look at me because the turning away made me think that she did love me. I only had to stop her from turning away. But then one day she turned away and never looked at me again.

The MELTING HEADS

Shortly after L— left me it seemed as though my entire person was reduced to being a weak ache of body so much so that I didn't hear poems anymore and I had no thoughts that went beyond understanding how to move myself through time and space. The only thing I felt was a mild ache in my bones that seems hardly worth calling an ache because in truth it didn't cause me any pain but simply made my body heavy as if I wore everywhere the lead apron given to me by an x-ray technician whose office I didn't remember visiting. So even to name the feeling I am describing as an ache is not accurate but I know no name for the weight I felt that was not the ache of any specific ailment but only the slight and constant annoyance of having a body.

And whoever had given me the bruise was sending me now a revisionary message but this time because I had never felt so alone I could no longer see anyone except myself in the shower room mirror or the brass doorknob so the new message didn't come through a dream or a poem but instead through a book that someone else had written. The book was a book I had found on one of the reading tables in the Periodicals Room as I was on my way to my seat in the Rockefeller Library. I had stopped to look at the book not because I had recognized the name or the author of the book but because I had seen the book out of the corner of my eye as I passed it on the table and the cover was a special cover that caught my eye. A cover that had three different paintings of a man's face melting on it and there was something that I had liked about the way the faces looked when they were melting and I think it was that the faces when they were melting looked not like faces of dripping paint but like faces of melting flesh and the flesh didn't look so much like flesh but meat. And since there were no faces really left in the paintings but only these melting heads of flesh that looked like meat there must have been something that I also liked about the fact that the faces weren't faces anymore but only heads made of meat. And even though in the book there were no more pictures of the heads of meat only the author's ideas about what it meant for this painter whose name was Bacon (which somehow seemed right for a painter who made pictures of heads that looked like meat) to make a picture a portrait of a person that turned the face into a head of meat I decided to read the book since the pictures seemed so right to me that I was willing to read about them even without being able to see them and though the book was a little bit difficult for me to understand especially without pictures to show me all the ideas about flesh and faces and heads and meat that the author saw in Bacon's paintings there was one idea that was easy for me to understand and it stuck with me and because it was easy for me to understand I thought that it must be an idea that I needed at that moment because I was so sad that L— had left me.

The idea that I liked so much was the idea that in the paintings the faces turn into melting heads because the faces are mostly trying not to be faces anymore and the faces are attached to bodies that don't want to be bodies anymore. What I mean is or what the author meant was that the people in the paintings are trying not to be flesh and blood any more and so the melting head of meat is just the first step in a long process of not being flesh and blood anymore and so the painter by being this kind of melting meat painter is helping the person's whole body begin to disappear. And so the book said that when a person is screaming in one of Bacon's paintings it's not exactly like the person is screaming just to scream—just to show that something hurts—but the person is trying to create an opening—a hole—for the body to slip out of itself. So when there is a painting with a melting head that is screaming the head is really trying to melt into and out of the open mouth and disappear into a sound so it doesn't have to be a body anymore and there was something about that idea that I really liked and I think that I liked the idea because it seemed to be the opposite idea that the bruise wanted to give me or that the poem gave me because it seemed to me that the bruise and the poem had made me try to become a face and a body when I had just been a head of meat waiting to slip out of my own mouth like an idea. But then the bruise came and the poem came and it seemed like all those things came to bring me back into my body so that I would finally kiss L— and finally become a person. But even though I kissed L— and let myself be a person in a body still L— left me and suddenly now it didn't seem so important to have a body anymore and it didn't even feel very good to have a body anymore. Even when I was with L— it was very confusing to have a body but even though it was confusing at least when I was with her there seemed the possibility that I wouldn't be lonely anymore but now that L— was gone it didn't seem very important to have a body anymore because the body just seemed to make the loneliness worse. So when I read this book even though I thought it was a message from the same person who gave me the bruise and the poem and all my dreams I wondered if it was really the same person at all and I thought maybe this was a message from another voice—a voice that was against the voice that gave me the bruise and the poem—a voice that didn't want me to be a person in a body anymore. And I thought maybe this new voice was a better smarter voice that knew it was better not to have a body but I didn't even know if all these signs came from angels or ghosts or voices or if all these messages were coming from different parts of me and with all the confusion it was impossible to know who I should listen to or what exactly I was listening to. But the idea that a body could no longer want to be itself so much that it could scream just to fall out of itself seemed like a real idea to me and sometimes late at night when I couldn't sleep because I was thinking too much about how it felt to sleep next to L— I would open my mouth and although I wouldn't scream I would keep my mouth wide open until I fell asleep just to see if suddenly my body would slip out of my mouth in the middle of the night and I would become something else but I never did. And I liked the idea that even when the person in the painting was too tired of being a person to scream and free himself that even when he was so tired that he had to lean over a sink in the painting that the flesh was still willing enough to melt even though there was no mouth to melt through and the sink knowing that there was no mouth for the person to fall through let the melting flesh fall and escape down the drain. The drain was there for the flesh to fall through so that the person could finally disappear from the world and no longer have to be himself.

And the more I read about how Bacon liked to turn peoples' faces into heads of meat so they could melt away and not have to be people anymore the more I wondered if when he walked down the street and looked at peoples' faces if he could actually see how much the people didn't want to be in their own faces anymore. And then I wondered what it would mean to see a person's face and see how much the person didn't want to be in her face and so because the face showed so much how it didn't want to be a face the person looking at that face would not see the face but only see this melting head of meat that was really the first step in helping the person escape her face. And when I thought about that I began to think that the painter was almost like a saint saving people from the flesh and helping them become part of the spirit world faster and if he only could do in real life what he did in his paintings there would be so much less sadness in the world.

And in the mornings after I hardly slept because I missed L— so much I wondered while brushing my teeth in the shower room if the horrible feeling that I was feeling in my body because I was no longer with L— I wondered if the horrible feeling was actually my flesh not wanting to be flesh anymore and I wondered if I leaned there on the sink long enough if

I would just melt down into the drain and disappear into the spirit world. And because I never fell out of my mouth at night or down the drain in the morning even though I felt like I didn't want to be a body anymore I began to wonder if the idea that Bacon was painting was actually an idea for real life or just an idea for paintings. And since I hadn't even really seen any of the paintings but only read about them in the book I thought maybe the idea wasn't even an idea that worked in paintings and I wondered if when I actually saw the paintings of the scream and the sink if I would really look at the paintings and think that the bodies were really trying and wanting to melt out of their own flesh. And the less I melted when I wanted to and the more I thought about this idea I wondered how it would even be possible to have a painting that could really show this idea and maybe the idea was just the idea of the author of the book—an idea that he had while writing about the paintings after not looking at them for a very long time because I knew that it was easy to write anything that you imagined with words because words could say anything especially when a person just started typing with a small idea and let the words take over the idea. But I wondered if a painting could really show that a person just standing over a sink was really a body that wanted to melt and fall down the drain of the sink. And so the next time I went back to the library I went to the card catalog and found a book with pictures by Francis Bacon and when I went to the third floor into the stacks and found the book and opened it the first picture I saw was not one of the pictures I had come to see. It was not of a man screaming or of a man leaning over a sink waiting to melt down the drain but it was a picture of a man sitting. The picture was of a man sitting on a white table with wooden legs. A table that was long enough to reach across the painting left to right. And it was impossible to say where the table was exactly except in the painting because in the painting there was nothing but a color for a background. A bright orange color. So it was impossible to tell where the table was exactly because the background was not a specific place but just a color and not a place—a very beautiful bright orange place that was not a place. And the man on the table was sitting in such a way that his right leg was extended in front of him and that leg was a horizontal line across the middle of the painting—just as horizontal as the table top. And the other leg—the left leg which was deeper in the painting because the figure was extending his right leg from left to right in the painting—was bent into a V and the man's arm was clasping the bent leg right below the knee. And the head of the man was turning into the painting so that I couldn't see the face of the man just his back and on his back there was a very deep cut and the deep cut was the first thing I noticed when I looked at the painting and when I saw the deep red cut that looked like a long red gash I immediately imagined the rest of the man falling into the cut as if the cut were like a drain and I imagined the whole man disappearing and there being nothing left in the painting except the table the beautiful orange color and a floating red mark that used to be a gash in the body but was really a gateway to a whole other universe where flesh no longer had to be itself and when I thought all these things I remembered that I had thought them all because I had just read a book that had said all these things almost and so I began to wonder if I actually would have thought these thoughts if I had never read the book about the paintings. I wondered if I would have thought these things if I had only just seen the paintings and so I closed the book of pictures and opened it again to see if a picture was as strong as an idea about a picture and when I opened the book again I saw the same thing. I saw the entire body wanting to slip out of itself through the long red gash in the man's back and because I could see the want so much I could also make myself see what wasn't happening on the painting and one more time I saw the whole body falling into the cut on the back and disappearing. And again in my mind I imagined the beautiful painting that was just the table and the lovely orange color and the beautiful red gash floating by itself in mid-air with no body to hold it anymore and I wondered what would have happened to me if the bruise on my forehead hadn't been a bruise on my forehead but a deep cut on my back.

The HUM

The first time I heard the hum I was standing in the shower room with my head sticking out the window waiting for Pam to come. It was already dark when I saw the silver body of the car drive slowly down the street. It turned into the driveway of the parking lot. I could feel the bottom of the window frame hitting the back of my neck and the air against my face. My head was almost in the trees. The hum came from behind the trees. It was coming from the streetlight. From inside the silver casing where the bulb burned so white it didn't look like anything held in a ball of glass but like the picture of a ghost I had once seen. A light so white it was almost nothing. When I looked at it carefully through the trees I could see it get a little bit larger then a little bit smaller. I could see it never stop moving.

When I saw Pam get out of the car I thought for the first time that school was a place I could leave. I had never thought that before but she had come from far away to visit me at school and because I saw her get out of the car I could imagine her getting back in the car. I could imagine her getting back in the door and closing the door and turning on the engine and checking to make sure there was no one behind her. I could imagine her backing out and so I could imagine her leaving. And because I could imagine her leaving and she was someone who had come to visit me at school from the place I had left in order to come to school I could now imagine leaving. And though I couldn't imagine myself going back to the place I had left in order to come to school I could imagine myself now leaving school and going someplace else. I just didn't know what other place there could be to go to. It seemed that I had never been anywhere except school. And even though I had walked to the river with L— and slept in L—'s house far off campus there was a way that my time alone with L— was still a way of being at school—a way of hiding but never leaving—so that I still in my imagination was always at school because there was a way that the river and L—'s house because they were a way of being at school when I couldn't be seen at school were also in my mind part of being at school. And so when I saw Pam's car pull into the driveway and it made me imagine leaving school forever I thought to myself that leaving school was something that I had never imagined before.

It was strange that I heard the hum that night—the same night that I thought about leaving school for the very first time. It was strange because when I finally heard the hum I knew that it had always been there. The hum was strangely not strange at all because when I finally heard the hum it was less as though I was finally hearing the hum and more as though I was finally admitting to myself that I had always heard the hum—that the hum had always been there in the background. And once I heard the hum I heard it everywhere. I heard it in every overhead light from the dormitory hall and shower room to the overhead light in the library right above my seat. Outdoors the hum came from every street lamp and all the lamps lighting all the walkways across campus and when during the day the lamps lighting the walkways were turned off though the hum was much fainter I could still hear it if I listened carefully coming from every heating and cooling unit attached to the back of every building. And even when I was alone in my room where I had always been careful to never turn on the overhead lights not because I had always heard the hum but because I had never liked the harsh light they emitted and so I had always only used several small reading lamps brought from home to light my room even there where I had no way of hearing the hum directly I could still hear the hum's gentle vibrations through the floorboards from the overhead lights on the floor below me and I could hear the hum coming through the door that led to the hallway where the overhead lights were always on.

But the first time I heard the hum was when I stuck my head out the window of the women's shower room when I was waiting for Pam. It was strange to see Pam pull up in her car because she stepped out of the car into the hum and because she hadn't existed always inside it but only stepped into it I knew that even though the hum held my body and I lived in it and I had lived inside the hum ever since I had come to school I like Pam could exist—if I ever chose to—outside the hum. And though when I first thought about stepping outside the hum I wondered for a second if stepping outside of the hum would be like stepping outside of myself I didn't wonder about that for very long. Somehow I knew suddenly without much thought that I existed separately from the hum though up until that moment when I saw Pam's car pull into the driveway the hum was no different than the noise in my own head. But when I thought about the hum as I stuck my head out the shower room window I also thought to myself that I was naturally separate from the hum—that I was not the hum itself. After all I had been other places besides school but it wasn't until that very moment that I was conscious I had existed other places besides school or that I could exist other places besides school.

I didn't hear the hum at first because it wasn't very loud and it hadn't started at a particular time but was already going before I got to the window and even to get to the window I had to walk through the shower room where the hum was coming from the overhead lights and before even getting to the shower room I had to walk through the hall where the lights also rang with the hum and even before I entered the hall I had been reading in bed in my room where the floorboards vibrated gently with the hum and even the door couldn't completely block the hum from the hall. And once I was in the shower room with my head out the window though I had my head out the window for a long time the hum didn't get louder or softer and it didn't start or stop. It was not something that would have been easy for me to hear. It sounded like nothing. So it's difficult for me to know why exactly I noticed the hum at all that evening.

But when the car came down the hill softly like a boat and took a wide turn where the driveway opened up into the lot right below the window and the trees I was standing there with my head out the window and the back of my neck pressed against the bottom of the windowpane and I could feel the old paint flaking and sticking to the back of my neck which was getting sweaty from being pressed against the old wood and my arms were getting tired from leaning on the sill. It was when I heard the soft sound of Pam's engine that I turned my head in such a way—I turned my head in such a way that I stopped looking straight ahead where the streetlight was—where I had been watching the bright light in the streetlight dance like a ghost—I moved my head to the left and down towards the driveway. That's when I heard the hum—when I turned my right ear towards the trees and towards the lamp directly in front of me. It was quiet but something about the motion of my ear made it just a little less quiet than before and that's when I stopped seeing the light move inside its casing and started hearing it. I heard it and I knew I was hearing it.

Pam's headlights shot long across the asphalt into the trees but the car drove to catch up with them and when Pam found a spot for her car right below the shower room window the headlights flattened and tightened against the brick of the building. The engine had been making a low but rumbling noise and now it wasn't making any noise at all. I could hear the hum better. And because I could hear the hum I forgot that Pam was down there and I should call hello to her. I forgot even though I could see her. That's how distracted I was by the hum. I was watching and listening to everything as if I weren't there. She turned the headlights off. The low branches of the trees were very close to my face.

I brought my head back inside the window and peeled the flakes of paint off the back of my neck. I could see Pam through the trees and the windshield. The streetlight lit her too. I was thinking about the hum and how it was behind everything. She turned her head to the side and put some things that were on the passenger seat into a plastic bag. She came out of the car. But before she came out of the car the door made a creaking sound. The kind of creaking sound that metal makes. Like a giant screw turning. A large dry screw. Before she looked up I closed the window.

When I opened the heavy wooden door—the back door of the dormitory—it creaked and when I stepped outside I could hear the hum again. When I felt the air I knew it was almost spring. I looked up and the trees were above me and the streetlight lit them from behind. I was wearing my plastic shoes. I could feel them hard against my heels. When Pam said *Hello* I said *Hello*. She put her hand on my shoulder but I didn't move. But I noticed when she touched me that I couldn't hear the hum.

In bed against the darkness of the room I could hear it inside of me. Pam slept oblivious to the hum next to me her face practically pressed against the wall. Her breath bounced steadily against the plaster. I could hear it now as if it were inside me and maybe it was. The hum echoing an emptiness as if my rib cage were a house made to hold nothing.

DAPHNE

What changed everything at the end of that year were some pictures of a sculpture shown to us in art history class and part of the reason that the pictures were able to change everything was that I saw them not in a book but in the dark projected onto the wall. If I pretended that each different slide of the sculpture was not a different slide of Bernini's *Apollo and Daphne* but just the different way I now would see the sculpture if I were walking around it in real space suddenly it was as if I were looking at the real sculpture itself and I wasn't at school anymore but halfway around the world in a Roman gallery.

And because the sculpture was of only one small moment in the bigger story of Apollo and Daphne the sculpture showed the moment when Daphne just began to change—the moment when she was not yet a tree but not quite a woman anymore. There was a way that the sculpture made me see much more than it really showed me. Because Daphne was at that particular moment not all woman and not all tree when I looked at the sculpture it was as if she were both a woman and a tree and also not a woman or a tree. I could see enough of her flesh to know that just a moment before this one Daphne had been a woman. But now there were leaves growing from her fingers and her arms were stretching toward the sky as if they too would in the next moment which I also would not be able to see—they too like the fingers which were now leaves would become something else. Branches maybe. But they were only arms now and Apollo's hand was pressing into Daphne's stomach but I knew when I looked at Daphne—because her stomach stretched just like her arms towards the sky—that despite Apollo's hand her stomach in the next moment which I knew I also couldn't ever see would become a trunk maybe. But now her stomach with Apollo's hand upon it was just a stomach so Daphne who was also not a woman was also not a tree. But because leaves grew from her fingers while Apollo's hand wrapped itself around her stomach I also knew that Daphne would in the next moment be a tree and in the moment just before this one she was a woman. And so in some strange way I thought she was also a tree and also a woman and it was because the picture of Daphne in the middle of her metamorphosis—the picture of her as part woman and part tree—could make me imagine Daphne as a whole woman as well as a whole tree. The sculpture had a special kind of magic that could make me see what was not yet there and what was not there anymore.

And even though I didn't think that it was possible in real life for a woman to actually change into a tree when I was looking at this sculpture of a woman becoming a tree still I had to acknowledge that Apollo's cloak billowed in a breeze that wasn't even there in the gallery and I thought to myself how soft and light the cloak is and then I remembered that the cloak was made of stone. And then I had to think to myself how impossible it must be to change a stone into a cloak that is soft and bends and billows in a breeze that isn't even there. And although it seemed impossible for a woman to become a tree still I had to say to myself here is a cloak that is made of stone and the impossibility of turning a piece of stone into a cloak is not unlike the impossibility of turning a woman into a tree. But the sculpture showed me that a stone can be turned into a cloak and that was somehow like showing me that maybe a woman could also change so much she could become a tree. And suddenly as I stood there looking at the sculpture all change seemed possible because the sculpture made me change the words in my head from cloak to tree and from stone to woman. And although the sculpture couldn't turn the woman into the tree right in front of my eyes the sculpture was enough to move my mind to imagine making a woman into a tree and so the woman became a tree in my own mind.

And so I knew that things could happen in the world as long as I could imagine them happening first and so I went back to my room that day and I wondered about all the things that I wanted to happen to me and how I wanted now to leave school forever but how I hadn't yet become a person who could leave school forever but I knew now from the sculpture that I had to imagine first becoming a person who could leave school forever and since I was not a person who could make sculptures out of stone to help me imagine things I did the only thing I knew how to do to help me imagine things so that I could finally leave school forever and I began writing a sentence to begin this book that was the beginning of me imagining leaving school forever and the sentence went like this: *If I had actually spent any part of that first night asleep, it is difficult for me to know now, though no more difficult than it was for me to know then.* And now that I have finished writing this book that started with that sentence though I have not been at school already for a very long time I hope now that I can finally leave school forever.